Speechless

Speechless

*

ADAM P. SCHMITT

CANDLEWICK PRESS

First paperback edition 2021

Library of Congress Catalog Card Number 2018960057
ISBN 978-1-5362-0092-8 (hardcover)
ISBN 978-1-5362-1901-2 (paperback)

21 22 23 24 25 26 TRC 10 9 8 7 6 5 4 3 2 1

Printed in Eagan, MN, USA

This book was typeset in Minion Pro.

Candlewick Press
99 Dover Street
Somerville, Massachusetts 02144

www.candlewick.com

To our boys, Aidan and Anderson

I'm about to learn the following:

1. Family members will be the first ones to make you feel out of place.

2. Family members will eventually show their true colors.

3. Friends and relatives show support in different ways.

4. Everyone has a breaking point.

5. Poor social skills can get amplified.

6. Some people enjoy a wake like it's a wedding.

7. You'll be surprised at who shows up.

8. You may hear things you didn't expect.

9. If you're not sure what to say about the deceased, don't share your thoughts.

10. Everyone has a story—especially the quiet kids.

11. If you're not sure what to say about the deceased, say it into a microphone.

12. Listen more than you speak.

*CHAPTER 1

Family members will be the first ones to make you feel out of place.

So this is it.

This is how I go.

Not in a fiery blaze of glory.

Not risking all of my being for a cause both mighty and true.

Not in any way that will be celebrated.

Pants.

These pants will be my undoing.

No way the few threads keeping that button on will hold for the rest of the day. Or tomorrow. No chance. Maybe if I just don't eat anything, they won't be so tight.

Painful red indentation lines have already formed under my muffin top. The pants are merging with my skin. I'm one deep breath away from losing them.

It's not like I ever asked for fancy dress pants. Mom bought me these for the spring dance in seventh grade, and they fit fine *then*. I know I've grown since last year, but maybe was in denial about my waist expanding with my height. These are the only black pants I own, and Mom said there wasn't time to get me new ones before the wake. And they would have to do. And that was that.

These pants may kill me.

At least I'm already at a funeral home. That should save everyone some hassle.

I need to get out of this car. Sitting only makes the pants more constrictive. We're the only ones in the parking lot, so at least no one will see if my waistline causes a scene. I step out carefully to keep the button from popping. Standing helps some. My skin gets a moment of relief as I run my thumbs between my waist and its tormentor. We walk to the entrance, each of us in our shiny shoes, with seemingly extra-loud footsteps against the pavement. I wonder if everyone thinks that when they walk into a wake.

The outside of the funeral home actually looks like . . . a home. A big white house with a parking lot. I know I've been by this place several times, but I never made the connection that it was a funeral home until now. It isn't how I pictured a place with dead bodies should look. And the man opening the entrance door to greet us isn't what I pictured, either.

"Hi, folks! Come on in! I'm just heading out, but Marty's on his way to join you."

He's . . . excited? I didn't expect this greeting, or the funeral director to be wearing a cherry-red baseball shirt with EMBALLMERS in gleaming white across his chest.

"Big day today. Chamber of Commerce season opener this afternoon. Every year we are sooooo close to the championship but never seem to get out of the playoffs. Not this year. Things are clicking for us, and this will be our season."

I'm not sure what I expected walking through the doors into my first wake, but an easily excited softball-playing mortician is a bet I would have lost.

"Uh, " Dad responds, trying to get his bearings on this guy, "good luck to you, then. Listen, I know we're early, but we were wondering if we could just set up a few—"

"Pictures! Sure! We can help with that. Shoot . . . I'm glad you said that. I was about to leave without my good camera. The wife promised to get pictures of the team. Should probably bring my coat, too — not exactly softball weather lately. Can you believe it's March and we still have this cold? Crazy, right? Going to make for a long seven innings. At least it's warmed up some since the weekend."

"So, we just need to get a few things set up," Dad says a bit more assertively.

"You know we've lost to the Sons of Pitches for the last three years? We're going to take them down today, though," he boasts, waiting for our approval.

"Can we set up for our nephew's wake now?" Mom interjects. She's done with this man.

"Oh, sure, sure. Let me just see where —" He places his hands on his hips while bobbing his shoulders around. "Marty should be here any second. . . ."

I don't know that this guy can focus on anything other than his upcoming softball season. May as well have fun with it.

"So, what's the strength of the emBALLmers? Pitching? Defense? A fierce lineup that can go yard?"

The mortician stops searching for Marty and looks

at me as if I'm the coach who just called him in to pinch hit for the win.

"Oh, we've got it all! Our cleanup hitter absolutely killed it last season. He's a machine. Our leadoff guy is Mr. Reliable, and our catcher can throw anyone out. It's going to be such a great season."

He's positively glowing. Any sense of empathy for a family about to bury a child has been replaced with sheer anticipation for his upcoming seven innings. How does this guy work with dead people? Or live people who are here to mourn dead people?

"Wow," I respond with a toothy grin. "You guys are going to have an awesome day. I, on the other hand, will be —"

"Jimmy, we need to get set up." Mom cuts me off before I can bait the emBALLmer any more. She knows I love toying with people who don't get it.

"Hey, there he is! Marty will take care of you folks. Wish me luck today!"

"Good luck, sir!" I respond cheerfully. I envy this chipper grown man whose love of his sport outweighs reading his customers. He gets to play seven innings of softball; we get to attend the wake of a thirteen-year-old boy. "Knock 'em dead!"

5

Mom gives me the familiar glare to knock it off.

"What? Can't I wish him good luck? It's an important day for the emBA —"

"Jimmy." Dad's warning tone lets me know he's done with my game, too.

The other mortician hurriedly greets us. No softball uniform: his suit is a serious black that matches his hair.

"Good morning. My condolences," he says while extending his hand to Dad. Not sure how he combines a sunny phrase like "Good morning" with a somber "My condolences" and doesn't sound weird, but he pulls it off. I guess when you do this for a living, you get good at that stuff.

"I'm Martin. We spoke on the phone yesterday. However I can assist you, please let me know." He looks younger than Dad and smiles with a mix of confidence and caring. I always pictured a funeral home employee like Dr. Frankenstein's assistant or someone old with wavy hair and a lazy eye, not this guy. I didn't expect Mr. Softball Superfan either, though.

"Good morning," Dad replies kindly. "We're the boy's aunt and uncle," he adds while tilting his head at Mom. "My wife, Lily," he says with his far hand on her shoulder to guide her toward the introduction. It reminds me of when we were taught how to lead our partner in the ballroom dancing unit of PE. Mom shakes his hand before it's my turn. "And his cousin, Jimmy."

"Hello, Jimmy. So nice to meet you," he expresses with concern while shaking my hand.

"Mortician Marty . . . great to meet you."

For someone not at all athletic, Mom puts a stranglehold on my arm ninja-quick. Message received. Two words come through her lips that are meant for me alone, but everyone gets to be part of hearing: "Not. Now."

Dad quickly intervenes before I get the chance to respond. He focuses back on Marty before giving me another chance to test him. "Is it all right if we set these up before everyone arrives?"

Mom put together two poster boards of pictures. She spent most of yesterday afternoon looking through our photos, letting out subtle bursts of profanity along the way. It isn't hard to find pictures of my cousin, but those when he smiled? That's a different story.

"Of course, of course. Let me gather a couple of easels for your display, and we can set them up next to the guest book." Marty opens his hand, gesturing toward a podium in the corner where a white book lies open with a silk ribbon down the middle. I envy his calmness.

We follow him through the entryway to a large, open room. It reminds me of an art gallery we saw on a field trip last year, only missing all the art. Patrick's body is on display at the far end. The room is just dim enough that the light above him acts as a spotlight. I would have done the opposite, but it's my first wake, so maybe the dead bodies are supposed to be showcased. I quickly look away once I realize it's my cousin. And I'm not ready to see a dead body.

Dad, carrying the poster boards, continues to follow the mortician to the corner. I'm following behind him, but Mom grabs my arm with the same firmness she uses when we walk through the glassware section of Elliot's. I didn't even say anything this time.

"Jimmy?"

Mom has her serious eyes on.

"Tomorrow you get to do something for Aunt Rose and Uncle Mike."

I hate when I *get* to do things.

"What? Be a pallbearer?" I halfway want Mom to be impressed that I know this term.

"At the funeral tomorrow, you're going to say a few words about your cousin."

My eyebrows creep down.

"The priest asked for a family member to speak about him," she says with authority. "And we all thought you would be best." The *you* stands out, getting extra emphasis among the rest of the request.

Images of a large audience, silence, and an over-sized microphone flood my mind. I'm able to formulate one word.

"What?"

That's all I get out. Too many other words, like *public speaking, crowd,* and *speech* are warring for room in my head.

"It's not a big deal. Just say a few nice things about your cousin is all."

"A speech?" My voice. It's getting loud. "In front of everyone?" It's doing that high-pitched thing I can't control.

Her voice softens when she detects the anxiety in my response. "Just think of it like the presentation you did in English. Your teacher said you did a great job on it. You'll do fine on this, too."

My big presentation last week on *The Iliad.* . . . I

did do fine on it. I actually think I gave one of the better speeches in my Honors English class. Even got bonus points for choosing a classic instead of a modern book. Still, just because I'm good at public speaking doesn't mean I hate it any less. It terrifies me. I peed three times before second period that day. I didn't tell Mom that part.

"Why me? I mean, why not —?"

"Obviously, his sister can't do it, so that means you need to."

Well, yes, we all know Sofia can't give a speech.

"Why not Uncle Mike?" I won't even ask about Aunt Rose. She couldn't problem-solve her way out of a locked car without her twin or husband by her side.

Mom steps toward the poster boards Dad is setting up. She tilts her head from one side to the other to see if his placement is straight. I haven't seen the pictures she chose to display until now, and I'm not happy that one is of a six-year-old me crying at Thanksgiving. I don't want that picture up, but that battle is small in comparison with the current one and not worth fighting.

"It's going to be hard enough for your aunt and uncle as it is. You can't expect them to stand up in front of everyone and talk after what they've been through," Mom says as if it were common knowledge. I still don't get it. I'm not trying to be a jerk; I just don't know why it has to be me.

I respond using the kindest voice I can muster. "Why don't you do it, then?"

That isn't well received. I have her full attention now as her face inches closer to mine. Marty politely exits. I bet he can tell this is getting awkward.

"Your aunt asked if you would do this for your cousin, and you are going to do this for your cousin and that's that," she responds with her words firmly gripping me. She does her patented "turn before I can respond" move and focuses back on the pictures.

And she wonders why the two of us don't get along.

"I know, but —"

Her attention is back on me. Not sure that's what I wanted.

"But what?"

I make a sound as if the word "I" had more syllables, but only the first one gets out and it just sounds like a weird breath.

"Really? Now is the time you choose to not have something to say?"

How do I respond to that?

"I . . . I don't —"

"Your aunt needs us." Her teeth grind together; only her lips are moving.

I hate it when she does her "I am the law" thing. There's no coming out ahead when it happens.

"Aunt Rose can't do it?" I'm reaching now; I know that. She would never put her sister in a bad spot.

"And we are going to do everything we can for her," she responds, ignoring my suggestion.

She's angry. Dad can tell. He steps in before it gets worse. He knows that Mom and me in a conflict can get explosive.

"Jimmy, you don't have to say a lot. Just a few nice things about your cousin." Everyone has stopped calling Patrick by name and simply refers to him as *your cousin*. "Just think of a story about you guys playing when you were younger, something like that. Something simple."

Mom walks toward the entryway of the funeral home as Dad tries calming me. She's done with me. I shouldn't have asked if Aunt Rose could speak. Mom always gets so defensive about her twin. She acts like vulnerable Aunt Rose is standing beside her and I'm slinging insults that only she can deflect.

"But why me?" I ask with all the sincerity I can find. None of this makes sense.

"It's the right thing to do." He looks toward Mom while she puts another pen out for the guest book. His expression doesn't exude confidence that the only possible solution is for me to be the speaker tomorrow.

"But what do I say? I don't even know what to make up." The Trojan War wasn't the most engaging topic to talk about for fifteen minutes to my Honors English class, but at least I didn't have to invent anything.

"You don't have to make anything up. Just tell a story about you guys playing when you were little. Say something nice, or mention something you'll miss about him . . . maybe a game you played together." Dad's selling comfort, but he knows I'm not buying it.

"Like what?" My voice always cracks when I'm frustrated, and though it's not there yet, I can hear that crack only an octave away. My anxiety over public speaking is fighting with my anxiety over what I'll say. Either way, my anxiety wins.

I try to speak with confidence: shoulders back, chin up.

"I don't want to give a speech tomorrow." Fake confidence is better than no confidence, right?

"It's not a speech. You're just telling a story about your cousin at church tomorrow."

13

"In front of everyone? That's a speech."

There's that octave.

"I don't know, Jimmy. Just . . . just don't worry about it."

I hate hearing that phrase. People only say that when something isn't their problem. Frustration is in his voice now, too.

"Your aunt and uncle will be here any minute and they don't need to hear this. You're talking about your cousin tomorrow and it'll be fine." He clears his throat the way he does when he's finished talking about something. I sense he's as outvoted as I am. "Come on. We're here to say good-bye."

I start breathing a little heavier. This happens when something overwhelms me. Mom and Dad don't like that I self-diagnosed myself with anxiety, but they don't know how it feels. It feels like . . . like public speaking in a room full of people staring at you.

I don't move. I stay in the corner of the large seashell-colored room and watch my parents walk to the front. They stop in front of my cousin.

He's so quiet. Patrick typically wasn't quiet. That's how I know he's really dead.

He doesn't look like himself. I know it's him, but

he looks different. Almost as if someone made a stunt double of Patrick for this. I keep my distance. The thought of a kid's corpse is still unsettling to me. My parents kneel in front of the casket and bow their heads. Thankfully they leave me alone for the moment and don't force me to get close.

The speech.

No way out of it now. I'm going to speak at the funeral tomorrow. I have to come up with something during the wake today.

My first wake.

I have no idea how they work or how people act at them.

What am I supposed to say tomorrow? Dad said to just tell a funny story or talk about something we did when we were younger, but he doesn't get it.

There are no funny stories about Patrick.

He always ruined everything.

I hated the kid.

Patrick was the kind of guy who would kick your dog. And not to see what the dog would do but what you would do. I've actually seen him kick a dog. Maybe I should tell that story.

I want to ask Dad again, but seeing Patrick's body

lying motionless in front of my kneeling parents stops me. No one else is here in the funeral home yet. Just us, Patrick's body, and deafening silence. I so want a natural disaster to strike, anything to change the reality of this moment.

There's no use trying to argue anymore. This speech is going to happen.

What could I even say about Patrick? I always called him "When, Not If" in my head. It was always "When will Patrick Feeny ruin/break/hurt something? . . . Not if." There has to be some story I can tell from the time when we were really little.

My childhood memories of my cousin typically involve tears from someone other than Patrick. We didn't play many games together as kids. He didn't do well playing with others.

OK, there has to be something I can remember. Playing as kids, fun stuff . . . When was a time I played a game with Patrick?

I actually do remember one game from when we were pretty young.

Near-death experiences are hard to forget.

* * *

Junior Explorers. Not just the name of the class, but what the instructors called us each morning in the week-long nature exploration summer class for kids going into second grade. Mom read me the blurb from the park district catalog. All I heard was "animals" and "dangerous"—two words any seven-year-old boy would take for bait.

The class met each morning for a few hours at a local park. The first day I remember feeling out of place for not crying when Mom dropped me off. One boy with red hair and mismatched socks was sobbing and lasted only a few minutes before his mom gave up and took him home. Another kid cried through the first half of the morning. I've never understood why kids cry when their parents leave. I've always looked forward to the freedom.

A couple of high-school boys wearing matching red shirts with an outline of a bear on the front were the camp leaders. They were both named Zack and towered over our group of boys sitting cross-legged on the wet grass. Within a few minutes of starting, three of us had asked about the wild animals. The Zacks said we would see the animals tomorrow. We spent the rest of the morning talking about birds, which to me weren't very wild. We each had to find a pinecone, and even though we all found one right away, the Zacks spent the next hour telling us to "keep looking for better ones" while they sat on a bench talking. They showed us how to smear peanut butter on them and dip them in birdseed.

I didn't find it dangerous, but one boy did.

A freckly kid named Noah wouldn't touch the supplies. He kept his distance from the table containing the birdseed and peanut butter. He started shaking his head, saying, "I can't! I can't touch it!" until the Zacks gave up and told him he could just watch. He calmed down a bit and sat behind the rest of us while we finished our feeders. The Zack wearing glasses tried to get the group back together.

"Now you can attract and feed any kind of dangerous birds in the wild," he said with a halfhearted smile.

The pinecone bird feeders concluded day one of dangerous-animals camp. I feared the rest of the week would bring the same level of excitement. As we drove off that first day, I could see the Zacks talking, the shorter one shrugging with his hands up. They didn't seem too worried about making the camp more adventurous. Not sure they cared.

The morning of day two did bring a level of excitement. Just not the kind I wanted.

"Why is Patrick here?"

"Stop. It'll be fine," Mom assured me as she pulled in next to my aunt's car. "Aunt Rose thought this would be good for Patrick, and they let him join late. So just be nice to him."

"Why did you tell her about it?" I asked in hysterics, suddenly dreading the day ahead.

The week before, Patrick broke my scooter by trying to see how high he could jump it. He never said sorry. Aunt Rose did, but he didn't.

"This sucks" came out of my mouth without my realizing it.

"Jimmy! Enough with the language!"

"I . . . I didn't mean it."

That was the truth. I didn't realize a bad word came out. Didn't matter.

"Choose better words or we're going back home."

Mom hates swearing and considers "sucks" swearing. It's the quickest way for me to get in trouble. I hadn't meant to say it, but when she told me Patrick was joining camp, it just slipped out.

"Sorry," I said shamefully.

"He doesn't know anyone here, so you need to be nice," she reminded me again as we waited for Aunt Rose to finish talking to the Zacks. I wasn't the one who needed to be nice; she knew that. I stewed, knowing I had no options, while my aunt prepped the Zacks. Aunt Rose never just dropped Patrick off anywhere without giving the host a talk about his "free spirit."

My arms crossed on their own while I started imagining the week ahead. I was already questioning if any dangerous animals were happening this week. Now I would have to spend it with one. I huffed out of the car and took a seat with the rest of the Explorers.

Patrick spotted me and waved with his arm straight out and only his hand moving. He was acting like he hadn't broken my scooter a week ago. I'd have to wait until my birthday to get a new one, and he didn't care. I forced a wave back, not saying a word as he plopped down next to me.

The Zacks stood in front of us with a stack of white paper, boxes of crayons, and a worn backpack on the picnic table. I hoped there was something scratching to get out of that bag, but it sat quietly. Zack with Glasses spoke first.

"OK, Explorers, we have an adventure for you

today. An adventure that will take us into the woods," he said while sweeping his free arm in the direction of the wooded area to his left. His other hand held his coffee. "We are going exploring on a secret mission." This last part he said in a quieter voice as he hunched down.

Secret? I was getting interested. Short Zack took over.

"Explorers, we are going deep into the forest. We need to be careful, be alert, and stay together because of the many dangerous animals lurking in the trees," he exclaimed while making a claw with his hand. We were more intrigued now but still not sure there would be any danger for us.

Junior Explorers was held at Washington Park. It's one of Harper's larger parks — a few minutes from home and a place every boy in the group knew well. While it does have a wooded area, it isn't something you would call a forest by any stretch. Washington Park has been known to host birthday parties, cookouts, and various other family events. All of which involve kids running through the small patch of woods. We were all familiar with them and had never seen anything more dangerous than a ground squirrel.

Zack with Glasses grabbed the items from the table.

He set his coffee down and held up the paper in one hand, the crayons in the other. "Your mission today, Explorers, is to find the perfect leaf."

All the seven-year-olds groaned in unison.

Leaf rubbings. Every one of us had done countless leaf rubbings since kindergarten. We all knew the routine.

1. Find a leaf.

2. Place it under white paper.

3. Rub the crayon on its side over the paper.

It seemed like anytime the weather was nice, we did leaf rubbings. Anytime the teacher was in a bad mood . . . leaf rubbings. It was a rite of passage for kindergartners in the town of Harper to do at least six leaf rubbings before you could move on to grade school.

"Do we have to?" Patrick interjected. His personality had moments of usefulness.

"Well"— Zack with Glasses paused, thinking of his sales pitch —"you don't have to. But . . ." He knew we were on to him. Short Zack had come prepared, though. He reached for the backpack.

"This mission has a reward. The reward is in this bag. So if you don't complete the mission, you don't get the reward." He dumped the contents on the table in dramatic fashion. A heap of Fun Size Snickers lay in a pile for us to drool over. We were all on our knees, inching toward the prize.

All except Noah.

"I can't have Snickers. . . . I'll die if I do. I can't be around peanuts," he said with a squeak in his voice. Each of us showed the empathy of a seven-year-old boy by exclaiming how we would eat it for him.

"Then don't eat it," Short Zack told him as if he had ruined the party. He stuck his hand into the pile and pulled out the crown jewel of the group — a full-size Snickers bar. It rose above the Fun Sizes like a giant among men.

"Whoever gets the perfect leaf sketch gets the grand prize," he said while holding up the trophy we all coveted. "We're going to explore the woods for an hour and give everybody a chance to find their leaf. Then we'll do our rubbings, and Mr. Zack and I will judge who captured the perfect leaf."

We all stood up, with renewed energy at the thought of winning the grand prize, and formed the single-file line we'd practiced the day before. The Zacks took us into the woods, where we scoured the ground and trees for the perfect leaf. There were no wild animals, no sense of being in danger. Didn't matter. There was a chance to get a full-size Snickers bar, and that was enough to motivate us.

We walked the trail of Washington Park Woods in search of the perfect leaf. Then a second time. And a third. The Zacks stayed up front while each of us searched with the fear that someone else would spot the perfect leaf before we did. Patrick was particularly good at hearing someone say they found one and pouncing before they could reach it. He hadn't stopped talking since the candy-bar display. Patrick was easily excited by anything with sugar.

The Zacks told us to get three leaves each, which most of us did in the first pass. Then Zack with Glasses said to keep looking. According to him, we missed some good ones and needed to go back through the woods again.

We returned to the picnic table armed with our findings, each of us eager to prove we had the perfect leaf. Zack with Glasses gave us paper while Short Zack placed boxes of crayons among us. We worked diligently, placing our naked crayons sideways while carefully rubbing the paper. It took surgical precision to apply the right amount of pressure to get the structure of the leaf without the color overwhelming it. I was quite skilled at this and liked my odds.

After a few minutes, we set our creations in front of us while the Zacks came by for inspection. They spoke quietly for a moment as we waited with our hands on our knees. I had no idea what the criteria was for a perfect leaf, but I thought my chances were good enough to take home the grand prize.

"All right, boys, you each did a great job. Mr. Zack and I talked it over and we have a winner," Short Zack said while displaying the Snickers bar that would require both our tiny hands to hold. Patrick was rocking with anticipation as he bit his lip, hoping to hear his name. Patrick liked candy, a lot.

"The winner of the perfect leaf exploration . . ."

Each of us leaned forward.

"Is . . ."

We leaned farther forward, gripping our knees, with craned necks.

Short Zack paused until we almost tipped over. Our eyes widened and our hearts pleaded with him to call our name. He inhaled and released the winner.

"Jimmy!"

Clenched fists and painful grimaces. That's how seven-year-old boys show sportsmanship.

My grin was ear to ear as I stood up to accept my prize. I had no idea how they decided what made the best leaf, but I didn't care. The giant Snickers bar was mine. I had big plans for it, too. I would eat some of it that night after dinner and put the rest in the freezer for tomorrow.

I went back to my seat while Zack with Glasses walked around our circle giving the rest of the boys the consolation-size Snickers. Except for Noah; he sat on his hands when Zack with Glasses offered him the treat.

Patrick looked at my prize with envious eyes. I gripped it tightly. He would not ruin this for me. Even before he received his treat, he asked with frustration in his voice, "Can we eat it now? We can eat it now, right? You never said we have to wait, so we should just be able to eat it now!"

He was talking fast. Like happy-energy fast. He talked fast last week after he saw my new scooter. Right before he broke it. I hoped the Zacks wouldn't take their eyes off him.

Short Zack was gathering up all the supplies from

the morning and responded, "Eat up." The Zacks started talking about something a few feet away while putting all the crayons back in the boxes.

"Wait," Patrick said while holding his hand in the center of our circle as if there were an imaginary button to press in the middle. "I have an idea."

I found my shoulders leaning away from the circle of my fellow Explorers. None of the other boys knew Patrick. They didn't know what his ideas were like.

I knew. Just like I knew he'd made sure the Zacks were turned around before he said anything, I knew Patrick's idea meant someone was going to be in tears very soon.

"We need to eat these like real explorers." He looked at me with his aggressive eyes. "One bite. We all get one bite and that's it." There was a hostility in his voice that could intimidate kids who didn't know him. He had a way of commanding an audience.

Sounded simple enough: eat your Snickers by shoving the whole thing in your mouth. If you didn't, then you were a wimp. I was pretty sure real explorers from old times didn't eat this way — very sure they didn't have Snickers with them, either. It was no use arguing, though. The boys nodded and were willing to try it.

27

All but two: Noah, who had nothing, and me. Patrick ignored Noah and focused on me.

"Since you won, you have to take the biggest bite." This was Patrick being Patrick, creating a masterful plan to destroy something good that happened to me. I wanted no part of it.

I looked to the Zacks. They were still turned toward the parking lot, knowing we animals had been fed and would be fine unsupervised. I was on my own.

"No, I'm saving mine." It came out sheepishly.

My response was met with an onslaught of disapproval. I think every one of them was still mad they didn't win and wanted to see my victory ruined. The candy bar sat in my hand while I wondered how it could possibly fit in my mouth.

Patrick unwrapped his Fun Size.

"I'll go first. Watch." He shoved the small block into his mouth and choked it down before he had a chance to enjoy it.

"Now you go." He pointed to the boy on the other side of him while still swallowing chocolate. The boy followed orders by unwrapping and shoving his entire Fun Size in his mouth. Patrick had a way of making himself the referee in his own competitions.

The game continued around the circle, skipped Noah, and then reached me. I had no choice but to play.

"You have to do it now," Patrick reminded me.

I reluctantly unwrapped my prize and saw it reach from my palm to beyond the tips of my outstretched fingers. I couldn't imagine it fitting in my mouth. The boys all watched eagerly to see me fail. They knew just as well as I did that it wouldn't work.

"Go on! You can fit it in. Come on. . . . One bite!" Patrick said with the angry energy taking over his voice.

My mouth opened wide. My hand went for it.

I shoved one end into my cheek, as far as it could stretch. I figured it would choke me if the bar was forced straight back, so I tried to go sideways, like a bow tie for my teeth. Push and push again, and now a third effort.

I couldn't believe it. The entire Snickers bar actually fit. My mouth was two inches away from being able to close, and my cheeks were wider than my head, but I did it. I got a candy bar bigger than my hand into my mouth. The other boys leaned back where they sat, unable to hide their impressed expressions.

All but one. Noah looked like he saw something the rest of us didn't.

The moment of achievement lasted about two

seconds. Then I realized I couldn't swallow. I coughed, hoping I would hack the candy bar out. No, it only made things worse. My tongue moved in every direction, trying to pry the bar out, but I grew more frantic as the massive block sat wedged firmly in my mouth.

I coughed again. It only caused me to lose my breath. There was nothing in my throat, but I still couldn't control the functions of my mouth. It sent the rest of me into frenzied movements.

A tiny drop of spit hit the back of my throat.

Panic set in.

I stood up, clawing at my cheeks, as if that would loosen the bar, while my midsection bobbed up and down. I felt my eyes water and heard "He's choking!" come from one of the boys. I fell on my knees, coughing furiously, facing the ground.

I thought it was the end.

A hand grabbed me. One of the Zacks heard me.

Short Zack placed one hand on my shoulder to stand me up straight. I was wrong when I thought the candy bar was too big to fit in my mouth, and I was wrong when I thought Short Zack's hand was too big to retrieve it. His fingers struck like a cobra, too fast for me to see it or know what he was doing. One swift motion — that's all it took.

I didn't realize it had happened until I saw the chocolate block in his hand. He held it in front of me for a second — I think to reassure me that it was out of my mouth and I could breathe again. His hand never left my shoulder as he threw the Snickers to the ground and turned to his side.

"Thanks, Noah. Good work," he said as the freckly Explorer looked at me with concern. Noah had been here before. He was no stranger to someone reacting after putting something bad in their mouth. "You OK, Jimmy?" Short Zack asked.

I wasn't OK.

I couldn't speak.

I was crying.

I nodded anyway.

The Zacks had no idea Patrick had orchestrated the whole thing. They just thought I was a dumb animal trying to put big objects in my mouth. I pulled myself together as best I could before the parents arrived. I hoped the Zacks wouldn't say anything to Mom.

They gave us our leaf rubbings, and we walked to

the parking lot as our moms were pulling up. Patrick quickly got into Aunt Rose's car without even looking back. Short Zack talked to Mom, since my red face couldn't hide that I'd been crying.

He gave her the short version, but it was enough to make her furious with me. I didn't tell her the long version, the Patrick version. It would have only made things worse.

It was all my fault anyway. I was the one who shoved a brick of chocolate in my mouth. I was the one trying to not look like a wimp in front of everyone.

I was the one who did what Patrick told me to.

I promised myself to never listen to him again.

*CHAPTER 2

Family members will eventually show their true colors.

When you walk into a funeral home, this feeling happens. It's like when you walk into church . . . but scarier. You don't want to touch anything, you have to be quiet, and there are men in suits walking around watching you. It's like a boring museum, with tissue boxes every ten feet.

I don't know if sitting down at a wake is rude, so I do it before anyone arrives. One side of the room has a couple of large high-back chairs, while a couch is centered toward the back. I choose the more comfortable-looking couch, and my pants immediately remind me that I was better off standing.

Mom and Dad are still going over things with Marty in his office.

So it's just me and Patrick.

And silence.

And time.

I scan the room again for anything interesting. I don't want to look at the pictures of Patrick. I wish they had magazines, anything to distract me. The walls are bare of any art or decorations. Maybe it's too hard to pick out paintings that pair nicely with corpses.

Near the sign-in book is a narrow table with the room's only decoration: a pyramid of plastic fruit, painted gold, stacked in a matching bowl. At the top of the pyramid rests a perfectly shaped golden apple.

This is a bad omen. This is how the Trojan War started. The goddess Eris tossed a golden apple through Zeus's gates and said it was "for the fairest." Then the female gods started arguing, turning on one another. Things escalated quickly and didn't stop until the Trojan War. All because of an apple.

Is that where I'm headed? Some big ugly mess because of a little thing like a speech? It already feels like everyone has turned on me.

"Hey, pal, you doing all right?"

Dad. I knew he would check on me.

"Fine." He hates one-word responses, but I want him to know I'm mad.

"Look, don't worry about this speech. It's . . ." He lets out a breath as though it's a lot of work to find the right word. "It's just part of the service." Guess he didn't find that word.

"K." Down to one letter.

"It's just something you need to do. All right? I spoke at Grandpa's funeral. I talked about how we went fishing. I didn't want to talk in front of everyone, but I did it for Grandpa."

"So I'm doing this for Patrick?" I'm breaking my one-word rule for this opportunity to corner him. He's trying to make me feel better, but he knows just as well as me this isn't fair.

"Well, yes"— he knows Patrick's benefit is not a selling point with me —"but also for your aunt and uncle."

"If you spoke at your father's funeral, why don't they speak at their son's?" I'm pushing. I know it.

"Because it's going to be hard enough for them tomorrow. It's going to be hard on everyone. You were his best friend and —"

"Art?" Mom sticks her head out from the hall.

"Could you come to the office? We need to sign some papers."

I stop staring at the floor and look him in the eye. He knows I would never call my cousin a friend.

"Look, Jimmy. To him, you were his best friend. I know you don't see that, but you were." His shoulders turn toward the hall.

"Can you ask Mom if someone else can do it?" This won't go anywhere, but I want to at least hear the truth. I want someone to admit that no one wants to do it.

"Art?" Mom's voice commands again.

"Jimmy, please, we need you to do this. I can help you with it later."

"K." Back to one-letter responses.

Dad always takes the path of least resistance with Mom, especially when it comes to anything with her sister. I wish he stood up to her more. As he walks down the hall toward her voice, I am confident it won't happen today. At least he tries to help. A for effort; not so much for results, though.

Just me and the quiet again.

All I can think about is this horrific speech that no one else will do. What am I going to talk about? My speech on *The Iliad* was different. I like talking about

Greek mythology. I pick that topic every time we're given a choice. Something about the all-powerful gods behaving like spoiled children has always appealed to me. But this isn't the same as talking about a book. How long do I have to talk for? Will everyone notice I'm wearing the same suit?

Back to just me and the room — this intentionally plain room. If a furniture store and a dentist's office had a baby, this would be it. Open enough to accommodate a fair number of people, but without rows and structure — and a sense of anxiousness in the air.

The quiet is pierced when the metal handle of the entrance door springs back into position. I'm surprised a place like this has such a loud door. A woman's gruff voice cuts into the silence, followed by the clamor of the door closing itself.

"Good Lord, that's heavy."

She pauses at the entrance as if she's waiting for someone to greet her. She looks to be my grandma's age and about as pleasant. No clue who she is or whom she's talking to.

I turn back to the walls. She's Marty's problem. Being social and polite isn't in me right now.

All right, time to take advantage of the quiet. Patrick,

let's see, what to talk about . . . I could talk about the time we played hide-and-seek in the basement and he got stuck in —

"Well, this is certainly nicer than I expected," she says, this time directly to me while hovering behind the couch. "No need to get startled—just need my coat hung up." She lays her coat over the back of the couch, just enough in my personal space to make me uncomfortable.

Her feet remain planted behind the couch and her head swivels around. Even though Mom and Dad aren't my favorite people right now, I desperately hope they'll appear.

"I always get to these early. Best to beat the crowd. I can't stand for very long, so I'll pay my respects now." She squints at the casket until her eyes disappear.

"Yeah . . . I — I guess that's tough," I stammer back. Her arm extends toward me, her hat in hand, as if to display it.

"Where does this go?"

"Typically on your head," I respond without even thinking. She pauses long enough to look me up and down, then glares sternly, making no secret of her quiet judgment.

"I see. Wise aleck, huh?" she retorts with ice in her voice. I immediately regret saying anything.

"Uh . . . I . . . I'm sorry. I do that sometimes. I think your hat can —"

"Do what sometimes? Act like a jerk?"

I can't move. She has me locked down. I can't think of any way to respond to that. Who is this lady? I didn't mean to sound like a jerk. I don't think I'm a —

"Well?"

"Um . . ." is all I can get out before she starts up again. Oh, how I wish someone else were in the room.

"Same for my coat. Too warm to wear it in here. Just need it hung up somewhere for now."

I stand up, complacently getting her hat to hang it with her coat, a submissive act of kindness that will bother me later. I hate doing things just because I'm told to. I hang them on the rack that couldn't have been six feet from her still-planted feet. I'm already thinking about the ten different things I should have said to this strange woman giving me orders.

"And who are you?" she asks, this time as if I just walked through the front door of her home.

"I'm Jimmy," I respond politely. "I'm his cousin." I

figure that's what you say at wakes: how you know the person who died.

"Betsy."

That's all I get. So apparently not. She clutches her purse with both hands in case I am about to steal it.

"My, you're young. Didn't know he had a cousin your age. Maybe you were a secret or something. These things bring out all kinds of skeletons."

What's that supposed to mean?

"Uh . . . I guess." Please, let someone else show up.

"An awful shame nonetheless. Such a nice man and so young still."

Still? Not sure why that word sounds funny, even coming from my socially awkward acquaintance. Betsy is the first person I've met at the wake. I'm already clueless how these things work, and so far she is my role model for etiquette.

"Yeah . . . he was very young." I decide to just repeat the last thing she says until someone else comes.

"You greeting people at the door? You should be standing if that's your job."

"Um, no. I was just —"

"Then someone should be greeting people at the door." That callous tone and quick delivery to tell others what they should be doing reminds me so much of my grandma, and in no way does that comfort me. She turns her attention back to the casket.

"I remember seeing him at Grace's service last year. Looked healthy as a horse. Shame."

Grace? Who was —?

"Still had that limp, but you could hardly tell unless he was —"

The door. The metal-on-metal clamor I previously found unnerving is a welcome sound. Someone else is here. I don't care if I know them; any interruption from this woman would be better than being alone with her. My smile grows on its own when Uncle Mike steps through the entrance.

"Hi, Uncle Mike!" comes out of me excitedly. I'm so relieved to see him.

"Hey, Jimmy," he replies with a forced quarter smile and tired eyes.

I'm an awful human being. I'm so happy to see him that I forgot why we're here — to bury his son. I so badly want to go back in time ten seconds and not sound happy.

He holds the door for Aunt Rose. She takes a large breath when crossing the threshold while tightly clutching what looks like a photo album. Uncle Mike keeps the door open long enough for Sofia to walk in under his arm.

"Hi, Aunt Rose." This time I got it right and didn't smile.

"Hi, Jimmy. You look so handsome." The tears are coming. I have a feeling there's nothing I can say that won't bring on tears. She's a crier, but today is going to be especially bad. "All dressed up . . ."

She doesn't finish that sentence and instead strokes my arm.

I turn my attention to my little cousin.

"Hi, Sofia," I say, waving my hand, knowing her little arm will reply in the same manner. Sofia waves back with one hand while clinging to her stuffed walrus in the other. When we'd go to their house, I hardly ever saw Norman the Walrus. When they'd visit us, he was an extension of Sofia. Norman won't be leaving her grasp today.

"Well, I'm going to pay my respects," a voice interjects.

Betsy. Forgot about her.

As I was greeting my aunt and uncle before they say good-bye to their son, I forgot about this troll standing an arm's length from me. She might be sensing a line is about to form and makes her way toward the casket. Until now she stood with us like she were part of the family.

Mom and Dad must have heard the voices and make their way from the hall. Not sure why they didn't come when they heard Betsy's voice. Mom walks in first with a hug for her sister. Dad follows, looking like he's ready to move heavy furniture.

"You look so handsome, Jimmy," Aunt Rose says again, staring at me for a few more seconds as if there's something else she wants to say. "So handsome," she repeats, this time more to herself than me. She stops crying long enough to get the words out. Then the tears come again. For her, seeing me in my suit only makes it worse for some reason. I have no idea how to respond and hope one of my parents will step in. Thankfully, Mom hugs her again.

"Thanks, Aunt Rose." Should I say something else? I suddenly realize I never even told my aunt and uncle that I'm sorry about Patrick. I don't want to now. It would feel awkward in front of my parents.

"Morning, Art," Uncle Mike says to my dad as if it's

any other morning. I don't know what I expected. Uncle Mike isn't exactly a crier. My aunt does that enough for both of them.

"Hey, Mike," Dad responds in a similar tone. The two of them always use as few words as possible. He crouches down to the side of my uncle where Sofia's head is resting against her dad.

"And good morning to you, Sofia." Dad gives his greeting in a louder voice while waving an exaggerated gesture of hello. Mom and Aunt Rose are still hugging, gaining strength from each other.

Then a voice.

A voice yelling.

Betsy.

Betsy is yelling.

Betsy is yelling at Patrick's body.

"This isn't Frank!"

Mom and Aunt Rose break their embrace and stare at the woman. We all do.

"Who is this?" Betsy exclaims with the same social tact I imagine is used for kids playing on her lawn.

Uncle Mike opens his mouth like he wants to say something, but he won't look at her. He stands frozen, at a loss for words. He breathes fast, deeply, and stares at the floor. He won't even look in the direction of Betsy, who's standing right in front of Patrick. I don't know if he's ready to see his son.

Betsy scans our family and homes in on the only person she knows.

"Jimmy, who is this?"

Why did she have to remember my name?

I try to speak but nothing comes out. Dad takes a step toward her to take control.

"That. That's . . ." is all Dad clumsily gets out before she cuts him off again.

"Where is Frank? I came for Frank Riley's services," she tells the group like we got her deli order wrong. "Who is this?"

"H-h-he's . . ." Dad stammers out.

Aunt Rose, Uncle Mike, Mom, and Dad . . . none of them wants to address her. They all stop short of saying "Patrick."

"Well?"

"Pardon me, ma'am." Marty's calm voice breaks the room while he darts toward her. He moves with swiftness and is by her side instantly. "Mr. Riley's services are in the parlor down the hall. If you'll allow me to escort you to his area, I assure you the room will be yours to pay your respects in peace."

He's good, very good. It's clear he's been in this situation before.

"I wondered who this kid was," she retorts while walking away with Marty. "You should have a greeter to tell people where to go. I asked Jimmy here, but he had nothing to say."

Marty now has his arm around Betsy as they leave. I'll bet to her, his response sounds sympathetic. To me it seems as though he's moving her away as quickly as possible, without letting her even turn around. He's a pro.

We stand for a moment until we're certain she's gone. Her voice carries but sounds more distant by the second.

"Rose, is that the scrapbook? Would you like me to put it by the pictures?" Dad pipes in, trying very hard to sound as if the last two minutes never happened.

Aunt Rose hands over the large book, her eyes still focused on her son.

"I just spoke to the director. He said we have some time with him before anyone else arrives." He's speaking mostly to my uncle. My aunt is sniffling while Mom caresses her hand. "If you like, we can go to the other room so you can have time alone with him."

"No," Aunt Rose replies firmly, still gripping my mother's hand. "It's important to have family here."

Mom nods at her sister, then looks at me. "Jimmy, why don't you set the scrapbook by the pictures and show Sofia the other room. There should be some cookies in there."

I don't know if Mom did this for my aunt's benefit or mine, but relief floods over me. I knew all of us were meeting at the funeral home early to say good-bye to Patrick, but I wasn't sure what that meant or how it worked. I absolutely knew I did not want to do it in front of people.

Sofia is looking at the poster board of pictures, focusing on one in the center. It's a shot of my eighth birthday dinner, cut short because of Patrick. I don't think my birthday being ruined is why the picture stands out to her. It's what happened afterward, and how it changed her life.

I set the book down and hold out my hand for Sofia. She takes it with gratitude in her eyes. I step toward the hall when Dad puts a hand on my shoulder to stop me.

"Just give us a few minutes, OK?" Maybe he senses how unsure I am about how to respond to all of this. I nod in acceptance and watch Mom walk my aunt down the center of the room toward Patrick's body with Uncle Mike a step behind.

I smile at Sofia and nod toward the hall. I haven't said anything to her yet, but I will when we have a cookie with Norman.

As we walk to the cookie room, Betsy's voice carries into the hall telling Marty about Frank's limp. I had no idea that funeral homes had more than one wake at the same time. I wonder how many others have accidentally mourned the wrong person. She was right about the funeral home, just not the wake.

She was also right about me.

I had nothing to say.

"How many in your party?" the hostess asked, her head half-cocked, a welcoming smile on her face. She looked to be in high school and loving her job.

"Three tonight, please," I responded with my chest slightly puffed out. All day I had rehearsed telling the hostess how many of us there were. I pictured it in my head and made sure I walked in first and spoke loudly. I turned to my parents, expecting them to be surprised. Their newly crowned eight-year-old taking control like this had to be impressive. I got a different response when Mom corrected me.

"No, seven."

"What?" comes through my teeth as I exhale.

Seven. Four more than three. That meant my aunt, uncle, Sofia . . . and Patrick. This was *not* how I'd pictured it in my head.

"Who else is coming?"

I knew but wanted to make Mom say it.

"We always celebrate birthdays together — you know that. Aunt Rose wants to see you, and you know how much Patrick likes eating here," she said in her "Everyone knows this" tone when clearly everyone didn't know this. I think she held back on purpose. She knew I would have been mad.

"Why didn't you tell me he was coming?" I tried not to sound whiny, but it was tough. This was like having — exactly like having — your birthday ruined.

The hostess's bright-blue eyes shone with confusion. She still kept her smile. Dad chimed in, trying to smooth it over.

"Yes, seven tonight. And we have a birthday!"

"Ooooh," she replied while bending at the knees to come down to my height. "You must be the birthday boy. I have a special surprise for you. Birthday boys get to have the Super Sundae Bowl after dinner." I think she was more excited about the break in mood than my birthday.

OK, so this was pretty cool. The highlight of each Renaldo's dinner is the dessert. Not the dessert table or selection of pastries, but the soft-serve ice-cream station with two flavors. Each flavor dispenser is controlled by an ivory lever that requires the strength of both hands to operate. You can do vanilla, chocolate, or get fancy and swirl both flavors into your bowl.

To the left of the station is your choice of a cone or bowl. Kids always pick cones. It's common at Renaldo's to see kids cautiously carrying their way-too-high stack of vanilla back to their table. Sometimes they make it; other times they fly too close to the sun and their ice cream splatters on the floor. I was eight now, and done with cones. A bowl would give me the ability to manipulate my pour for maximum ice cream.

The Super Sundae Bowl, however, isn't available for regular customers to use as they pleased. This neatly pressed waffle-cone bowl (twice the size of the common-folk bowl) is reserved only for people celebrating their special day with Renaldo.

Getting one would make Patrick insanely jealous. That made me feel a little better.

The perky hostess showed us to our table, one of the few still open. Renaldo's buffet stretches from one end of the restaurant to the other. I'd had a plan in mind all day for my multiple visits to the food.

Plate #1 would be my warm-up. At the far end is what Uncle Mike calls the rabbit food — a section of lettuce with an assortment of dressings and toppings. The appetizers are next: wings, fries, tater tots, and my first stop, the nacho bar.

Plate #2 is always my favorite. The pasta station occupies more real estate than anything else. Each noodle can be drenched in whichever sauce you want. At the end of the station is the crown jewel of the pasta section: the macaroni and cheese. It's creamier than the box stuff from home and tastes so much better when scooped from the steaming metal tub.

Plate #3 is from where my parents usually go first. The meat station is what really classes up the place. Sure, there's fried chicken, but you can get fried chicken anywhere. What you can't get anywhere is freshly sliced ham. The chef uses his butcher knife and medieval fork to slice it to specified thickness.

Everyone can get what they want at Renaldo's. The rabbit food satisfies the dieters, the abundance of pasta and ice cream makes kids happy, and the dads get fresh-cut meat. This place has always made me smile. It's a magica —

"Hey, Jimmy!"

Patrick.

Just what I wished for.

"Hi, Patrick" squeezed out of my half smile. I didn't see the rest of them, but it was common for Patrick to run ahead of his family. I honestly didn't know how he hadn't been hit by a car yet.

"Hi, Patrick," Mom said. "You excited to eat here?"

Patrick responded with an impression of some kind of animal. It resembled a dog's movements but a tiger's growl, so I wasn't sure. It was just wild and crazed. Dad tried to make a guess.

"Whoa! Look at the hungry wolf! Hope there's enough food for this wolf," Dad offered, attempting to be funny. Patrick stopped his panting and pawing to correct him.

"I'm not a wolf. I'm Bobby the Pig. And I'm hungry!" he said between animal noises. I think he was trying to snort, and instead it came out like he was in pain.

Patrick did that sometimes. He liked to be other people or, in this case, an animal. Last summer he decided he was a king for a week and only responded if you called him "Your Highness." He also belched through dinner, ordered his parents around, and threw things he didn't like.

Aunt Rose, Uncle Mike, and Sofia came in and spotted us immediately.

"Hey! Happy birthday, big guy!" Uncle Mike said with a high five.

"Hi there, eight-year-old! I can't believe it! How's your birthday been so far?"

"Hi, Aunt Rose. It's been good. I got a new wa —"

"Food! Bobby the Pig want food!" Patrick had a charm about him that eliminated small talk. I actually didn't mind this time. I wanted to start my three-plate rotation just as badly.

Patrick loved buffets, and Renaldo's brought out one of his true talents: eating. He wasn't a big kid, by any means, but, wow, he could put food away. His insides must have had secret compartments or something. I had no idea how five plates of food could fit inside his wiry frame, but they always did.

We ate until each of us had at least two cleaned plates taken away. The dads made multiple trips to the ham chef, the moms took in the pasta, and Sofia cleaned out the fries. Then there was the pause. The pause that came when everyone's trip to the buffet had stopped and the only thing left was ice cream.

This was my time. The macaroni had created a soft cushion in me to catch all the ice cream I could eat. Thanks to the Super Sundae Bowl, it would be a lot. Dad walked to the blue-eyed hostess and pointed in my direction. She briskly moved to the kitchen and returned, holding the waffle bowl like it was a birthday cake. To me, it was.

"Here you go, birthday boy!" she said, placing the work of art in front of me. It was bigger than I expected and sparkled with a glorious display of sugar crystals.

"Look at that. . . . Let's get a picture of the birthday boy and his dessert," Dad said while rummaging for his phone.

"Bobby the Pig wants ice cream!" Patrick cried out, clanging his hooves on the table. My precious waffle bowl shook from the vibrations, and I gripped it like a wounded bird. "Ice cream! In a bowl like that! Now!"

Uncle Mike stepped in before the animal got loose.

"OK, OK, Patrick, why don't you go with your sis —"

"I'm Bobby the Pig!"

Uncle Mike clenched his jaw the way he always did when Patrick acted out. He was weighing his options.

I was done being polite.

"Go be a pig somewhere else. This is mine," I snapped without caring how it sounded. It was my birthday. Maybe being rude to Patrick was what I'd wish for. Mom quickly saw to it that wish wouldn't be granted.

"Jimmy!" she snapped with a glare. "That is not polite. If you want any ice cream at all, you will —"

"What? Act like a pig and yell at everyone?" This made no sense to me. I didn't do anything wrong, and somehow Patrick was the one she was worried about. It was my birthday. For once she could worry about me instead.

It was less than a second before she retaliated, but I savored that time as if it were my present.

"Jimmy! Enough! Your aunt and uncle came here to celebrate your birthday, and this is how you act?" Her eyes flashed with anger, but at least I'd gotten her attention. I'd learned at a young age this was the only way to get noticed with Patrick in the room.

"Me? How come Patrick's allowed to act like a pig?" I wasn't yelling, but I was getting louder. Aunt Rose put her hand on my shoulder.

"Patrick is just excited for you. That's all. He just gets excited," she told me as if I were the only one who didn't see it. "Let's all just get some ice cream and then we can hear your birthday wish. Sofia, Patrick, why don't you go ahead and fix your sundaes." She motioned to Uncle Mike for help. He was breathing heavily, his attention I'd fixed on Patrick.

Mom was still hurting me with her angry eyes. Fine. I wasn't going to say any more. I'd be in trouble later, but for the moment, I just wanted my birthday sundae.

"Just go with your sister to get your ice cream. Jimmy will be right with you," Uncle Mike said, trying to keep Patrick contained.

"Pigs are hungry! Bobby the Pig wants a bowl like that!"

Oh, no.

"That's it. You want any ice cream at all?" Uncle Mike's voice was getting louder, but I don't think he realized it. "If you do, you're going to listen to me." A lady sitting behind him turned in our direction. "Got it?" His hand was on Patrick's shoulder.

Patrick broke the grip and made his way to the ice cream. Sofia followed his lead.

"Patrick, be sure to help your sister," Aunt Rose calmly called out as her son ran away.

"I don't need help!" Sofia barked without even looking back.

I let the two of them go ahead while protecting my precious waffle bowl with both hands. Then Mom gave me the look that I knew well. It meant I had to pretend I wasn't worried that Patrick was about to ruin things.

"Go ahead, Jimmy. Go with your cousins." Her head was half-cocked like the hostess's had been earlier, but she wasn't smiling.

Oh, boy. Here's hoping.

I gathered my prize and held it close to my chest. With cautious steps, I made my way to the ivory handles of soft-serve delight. Sofia's bowl was already poured and overflowing on one side. Patrick hadn't been quick enough in helping her with the dismount. She did her best to fit as many gummy bears as possible on top and made her way back to the table. Patrick turned back to me.

"We need to fill it up with both flavors . . . this high," he said, his eyes wide, staring at my hands.

"That's all right. I just want vanilla."

That was a lie. I had every intention of making the perfect swirl, but I was too afraid Patrick would try to help and break my Super Sundae Bowl. "I'm just going to do vanilla and load up on hot fudge." That wasn't a bad compromise from my original plan.

"No! We have to try it! You only get those on birthdays and you've got to try!" I couldn't tell if he was excited or angry.

"Um . . . I just want vanilla, OK?" I looked toward the table for help. Sofia had all the adults' attention on her gummy-bear creation. I was on my own. Patrick had a hand on each of the levers.

"No, see? I'll pull both and you move the bowl really fast under them and then we can both share it!" He was getting louder. The ham chef straightened up and looked in our direction.

"I just want vanilla," I said again, with a little more force. This was my birthday. I wanted ice cream the way I wanted it.

"Bobby the Pig is hungry and wants both kinds in a

big bowl!" He took his hands off the levers and stepped toward me.

It was faint, but I could hear Uncle Mike call out "Paaa-trick" in that elongated way. It didn't help. It only turned more heads. Aunt Rose was still admiring Sofia's dessert creation. She wouldn't look, even though I knew she could hear Patrick.

"Use your own bowl. This one's mine!" I said, louder. This was my birthday. He was not going to ruin it. Unless he tried to grab my bowl.

Which he did.

"No! It's mine!" I yelled, gripping my waffle bowl with protective hands. Patrick grabbed it, too, and wouldn't let go. If I used any pressure, my Super Sundae Bowl would break.

"Let go! Patri—"

"I'M BOBBY THE PIG!"

The train had left the station.

Patrick clenched his fists, and with them went the structure of my Super Sundae Bowl. This time I heard Uncle Mike loud and clear. Everyone did.

"PATRICK!"

He didn't even finish saying his name before Bobby

the Pig showed his animal side. In a single motion, he spun, put his head down, and darted for the exit. He made it about three tables before his unstoppable force met a very movable object.

The hostess had walked over to help and was directly in the animal's path. Her feet left the floor like she was on skates, and the only thing that broke her fall was the silverware counter when the back of her head hit it. I pictured the blue getting knocked from her eyes. Dad jumped out of his seat to help her. She didn't move.

Uncle Mike ran after Patrick. Aunt Rose went after Uncle Mike. Sofia followed with her ice cream in hand. Mom went to help Dad with the hostess.

Everyone in the restaurant watched. I stood still, holding the crushed remains of my birthday.

One of the Renaldo's workers came out and helped the hostess to her feet. She wasn't able to stand on her own and winced with pain. Dad kept apologizing to her and tried to explain what had happened. I don't think she heard anything he said. Mom motioned for me to come over.

It was time to go.

"Come on, we're going to wait outside and let Dad

pay the bill." Paying the bill seemed to be a low priority compared to the injuries and mess Patrick had made, but I knew that was an excuse. She wanted to get out of there quickly. All the other diners' eyes focused on us while we made our way to the exit. Renaldo's suddenly seemed much larger — and the exit much farther away.

"Where did they go?" I asked once we were outside. It couldn't have been more than two minutes since Uncle Mike had chased Patrick out the front door.

"I don't know," Mom breathed out. "I don't see their car, so —"

"So Uncle Mike must have caught him?"

She didn't respond for a second. Then, looking at the doors of Renaldo's, she said, "I guess so."

Mom didn't like to talk about a Patrick aftermath. Any investigating on my end was always dismissed. But if I couldn't have ice cream, I at least deserved to know what was happening.

"Do you think Patrick will be in trouble?"

"I . . . I don't know, OK?"

I hoped he'd be invited to *her* next birthday. He could wreck it, then I could act like it was no big deal.

We got home and Dad poured himself a bourbon.

He usually does that when he's had a long day at work. I always know it's a good idea to busy myself in my room for a while when the bourbon comes out.

And then Mom and Dad talked loudly.

"There's something wrong with him! He doesn't just need a 'swift kick in the rear' like Mike thinks. He needs help!"

Bourbon isn't a whisper-inducing juice.

"That's not for us to say, Art! You can't tell someone how to raise their kids! You can't tell them they're bad parents!"

I'd heard this argument between Mom and Dad more than once. It usually ended with Dad saying, "It's only going to get worse," and Mom insisting he leave it alone. Not tonight.

"If Mike is too proud to help a kid that —"

"Too proud? He's a paramedic, for Christ's sake! He helps people for a living! You think he doesn't know how to help his son? You think Rose doesn't —?"

"I think your sister has her head in the sand all day and waits for someone else to fix everything!"

"Stop it! Rose works very hard and knows Patrick is a little hyper and ca —"

"A little hyper? That kid's off the charts! I wouldn't

be surprised if he has bipolar or something that he can't —"

"Oh, really, doctor? You have him all figured out? All kids get a little worked up sometimes. He just needs to —"

"He needs more than what they are doing!"

"You don't know that! You don't know if something is wro —"

"I know our son had his birthday ruined! I know that he's upset and didn't want Patrick there tonight! But, no, we can't ever do anything without your sister!"

I heard Dad storm upstairs — and Mom start to cry. That was the worst it ever got. I don't know how much further it would have gone if we hadn't gotten the call.

The phone rang twice before Mom answered. It was Uncle Mike. He was at the hospital.

Mom's crying turned hysterical. She couldn't even talk and gave the phone to Dad. He spoke slowly, focused. One word at a time.

"Yes" followed by "OK." Then the only complete sentence before hanging up: "But everyone is alive?" He put his hand on Mom's shoulder. I knew that whatever had happened was bad, but I was grateful it made them stop fighting.

"Jimmy, get Mom's purse for her. We need to go to the hospital."

"What hap —?"

"Now. I'll tell you in the car."

On the drive, Dad explained more. There'd been an accident. Uncle Mike said they were all alive and unharmed. By the time we arrived, he, Aunt Rose, and Patrick were finished getting checked out, but they were still waiting for Sofia.

They said she hit her head pretty hard. Uncle Mike said it was all his fault. I heard him tell Dad he was still yelling at Patrick to be quiet when he missed the stop sign.

While Sofia's head injury didn't cause any brain damage, it was enough trauma to have lasting effects.

She lost ninety percent of her hearing from her injury.

Had my uncle known that his words before being hit by that truck would be the last his daughter would ever hear, he likely would have chosen something other than screaming, "Shut up."

Uncle Mike never forgave himself for the accident that hurt his daughter.

He never forgave Patrick, either.

*CHAPTER 3

Friends and relatives show support in different ways.

The wake officially starts at one o'clock. I have this image in my head that since a wake is to respect someone who died, the doors will open to a mass of people waiting outside. But instead, like most parties I've been to, people don't show up right away. A few neighbors come shortly after one o'clock, along with some friends of my uncle's, but not many others.

Thirty minutes later, the wake begins to get crowded and everyone seems to know their place.

Uncle Mike, Aunt Rose, and Sofia are standing to the right of Patrick's coffin. Enough people arrive to form a line along the wall next to them. Mom and

Dad seem to be in charge of thanking everyone. They collect a group after they've paid respects to Patrick, thank them for coming, and wait for the next group. It reminds me of a checkout line.

I stay close to my parents and let them do the talking. I have no idea what you're supposed to say at a wake. People are now coming in faster than they're leaving. The sight of this traffic coming my way doesn't ease my anxiety or make my pants feel any less constricti —

"Hello."

I turn to see the owner of the familiar voice. Greg Karlov?

"It is good to see you, Jimmy. I am very sorry about your cousin. Please accept my condolences."

That's how Greg speaks. No contractions — and like he's been rehearsing lines off a script all day. He always struggled to make friends, but I don't think he cared. He acted as if he knew something the rest of us didn't, like our futures were all going to be awful and his wasn't.

"In case you do not remember, this is my father." He gestures to the man behind him.

I'm shocked he's here. Greg Karlov has been one of my classmates since kindergarten and is truly one of the weirdest people on earth. He wears camouflage something every day, and when he isn't in school, he's searching for fossils by himself in the woods. He was in my homeroom last year, but we don't even have any classes together in eighth grade. We're not friends. He certainly wasn't friends with Patrick. Really not someone I feel like being polite to at the moment.

"Hi, Greg. Thanks for coming. Hello, sir," I say to his father. His dad has that same look in his eyes as Greg does — a piercing stare that has always made me uncomfortable. Seeing Greg stand next to his dad is like seeing an apple next to an apple tree.

Greg extends his hand. He's one of the few people here who shakes my hand. "This was very sad news. I hope your family is getting through this all right."

"Yes, I mean, it's been a tough week." That's become my standard response for several of the short conversations I've had today. Most people follow that up with something about how they understand or they've been thinking of us. Greg and his dad just stare at me. Both with this practiced, polite smile, just staring.

"So . . . how've you been?" I ask.

What else am I supposed to say? It's bad enough I have to come up with a speech, but now I have to come up with talking points. I need to get away from this.

Greg responds first. "We have been well. It was a tough winter, but now we are doing well."

The confusion must show on my face because his dad steps in. "We lost Greg's grandfather just after Thanksgiving. You probably remember when he was absent from school for a week. Greg took it fairly hard and it made the holiday season a bit rough."

Great. I can't just walk away after hearing that.

"I'm sorry," I say, looking at Greg. I had no idea he was gone for a week of school. I don't think anyone other than the teachers noticed. "What did he die from . . . of?" I'm not sure what else to say. I immediately regret asking this.

"He had a heart attack," Mr. Karlov responds with his hand patting his son's shoulder. "But he lived a full life with no regrets. It was very sad, but not like this. Not like your cousin, taken all too soon." His head shakes. "So tragic." The head shake stops. "And I understand he was all alone when it happened?"

"Uh . . ." Guess I deserve that question since I asked first. "Yeah, he was alone. It's very sad." I want far away from this uncomfortable conversation. Mr. Karlov seems right at home.

"This is my first wake since then. It looks different

when you are just attending and not hosting." He looks around the room with genuine interest in being a guest at a wake.

"I bet." Back to more staring at me. I want to be somewhere else. "I have to speak at the funeral tomorrow."

I don't know why I share that with Mr. Karlov. He keeps staring, so I keep talking. "I have no idea what to say. I've never heard a speech at a funeral."

The eyebrows on Mr. Karlov's face go up. Not in a concerned or empathetic way — just interested, like he's curious about a science experiment I'm attempting.

"A eulogy. Yes, I spoke at my father's funeral. Have you got something prepared?" he asks as if he were a fellow scientist wanting to compare notes.

"No. I . . . I just found out this morning. I haven't had time to think about what to say." Mr. Karlov cocks his head but still keeps that stare. "Any advice?" I ask.

It's weird that I've somehow ended up talking to Greg Karlov and his dad more than any of my family in the room.

"How does one summarize an entire life in a few words? A difficult task for anyone. When I spoke of my father, I spoke of our time spent together, when he taught me my hobby of furniture making. I spoke of all I learned from him and how it impacted my life." He remains behind his son, his hands resting on Greg's shoulders. They both stare at me, waiting for my response.

Furniture making. OK. Never mind. This isn't helping. At all.

"That's good advice. Thank you." I can't do this anymore. I need space. "It was nice to see you both." I manage a halfhearted smile. "I'm just going to get something from the other room." I turn toward the hallway and begin to take a step when Mr. Karlov speaks up.

"Simply be honest. Tell everyone something you have learned from the deceased."

I stop for a second before continuing my escape. "Sure, thank you. Thank you for coming," I respond while walking away. Looking back, I catch Greg holding up one hand to give me a robotic wave good-bye.

Through the crowd and into the hall — that's where I can escape. Some kids are making their way in from the hall with the bathrooms. Maybe I can hide there for a bit and figure out a story to tell for tomorrow. I know Mr. Karlov was trying to help, but I don't think I've learned anything from my cousin.

I almost make it out of the crowd when I hear her voice.

We all do.

"All right. Who's here?" bellows from the entrance.

Mom's head turns first. She shows her teeth the way I do before getting a shot. Even with the noise of the crowd and kids running around, the voice rises above the entrance of the parlor. The words "Excuse me" come from Mom as she turns the rest of herself toward the person demanding attention.

Mom takes assertive steps to greet her mother, Grandma Mutz.

Mutz Lehmann isn't someone who walks over to people to say hello. People come to her, and they do so with purpose. Every time we see Grandma Mutz, there's an order to saying hello.

Mom's the first to greet her, followed by Dad or me, then whoever else happens to be closest. Family is always first, with friends and other acquaintances last. It's her law. No one ever saw this in writing, yet it's followed by everyone. Today is no different, as Grandma Mutz's Kleinsher loafers are pointed toward my mother.

As a newlywed in her twenties, Mutz worked a nine-hour shift six days a week at the Kleinsher Shoe Factory. For thirty-one years, she stitched leather on everything from men's work boots to formal wedding heels. To hear her tell it, she hated every minute in that factory. She also hated anyone who didn't despise their job as much as she did. When we went to Great-Uncle Bert's for Easter last year, we took the long way around the factory just so she wouldn't have to see it. Despite that hatred of Kleinsher Shoes, she wears nothing else. I've never understood that.

Mom approaches and hugs her tightly, her fist clenched on Grandma Mutz's back. It isn't because she's emotional; she's hiding her nails. Grandma Mutz doesn't tolerate unkempt nails. Mom gave up on doing her nails before seeing Mutz years ago. She had tried doing them herself, having friends do them, even went to a salon — didn't matter. Mutz has an idea in her head of what a married woman's nails should look like, and Mom has never gotten it right. Appearances are very important to Grandma Mutz.

Mom takes a step back so I can say hello.

"Hi, Grandma. Nice to see you," I politely say while giving her a hug. As I break away, she puts her hands on my shoulders and looks me up and down. I hate this part. I always feel so much smaller under her scrutiny.

While awaiting her verdict, I overhear "Mutz" and "Look, Mutz is here" from behind me. For a surly woman, she does have a fan base. I think people like to say her name out loud. Everyone in my grandma's generation seems to have a name that isn't the one given to them at birth. Her real name is Ethel, and how that became Mutz is still a mystery to me. I often want to ask the story behind it, but something always tells me not to.

"Very handsome, Jimmy."

That's it? That's not so bad. I'm used to hearing how badly I need a haircut or some other instruction on how to improve my appearan —

"But you should wear a belt with a suit."

And there it is.

"I know. I only have one and I couldn't find it." My belt would actually be pretty useful now. I could have the button undone and no one would know.

"Never mind the belt. So glad you're all right, Jimmy. To think you could have been out there with him when it happened. Can't even stomach it." She puts her hand on my hair, strokes it down once.

"Um . . ." What do I say? I wasn't with Patrick when it happened. Is she saying that's good?

"Hi, Mutz."

I step aside to let Dad in.

"Art," she says to Dad in a tone that could be either "Thanks for inviting me to Christmas dinner" or "I'm sorry your nephew is dead." Dad musters up a hello and digs in for the opening ceremony of criticism.

"Place is kind of small. You think it will hold everyone? When Shirley Bennington passed, they held services at McKenzie Brothers. Much bigger. And how's tomorrow going to work with it being so cold out?"

She'll give Dad at least two more points of criticism. Now's my chance to get away, undo the pants, and try to write something for tomorrow. I avoid eye contact and try to make a break for the guest book.

No one is signing in. Is it stealing if I rip a page out of the back of the guest book? Is this like church, where it's totally a sin? I don't have a choice. This is my only option for paper.

No one's looking at me. Pretending to examine the book, I clear my throat abnormally loud as the blank page rips clear. I probably just drew more attention to myself than if I had stolen the entire book. I'd make a terrible criminal. I grab one of the extra pens and hurry to the bathroom.

Finally, some quiet. The bathroom is all mine. I sit in the only stall, lock it, and soak in the ambiance of my tiny new home with no people.

"OK. Patrick."

"Patrick was . . ."

Nothing. I got nothing.

"Patrick was . . ."

Silence. Sucks.

"Patrick was my cousin." It's at least something.

What did Mr. Karlov say? Tell what I've learned? Or something like that — without the furniture making. Try to breathe. Just write what I've learned and be honest. Just put some words on the page and clean it up later. Just write.

Draft 1 of Speech

I learned early on that Patrick liked doing things outside. He was very energetic.

No matter what, I always tried to spend time with him. It wasn't always easy, since we had different interests, but we still found things to do together.

We always had fun, whatever we did.

The truth is he wasn't just my cousin — he was also my friend.

This is a horrific lie.

I can't do this.

The paper easily crumples in my hand, and I stuff it into my pocket. The stall suddenly feels much smaller, making my breathing much bigger.

I abandon my newfound escape and plow back into the crowd.

Grandma Mutz is still talking to Dad, pointing out things she dislikes about the room. I don't think Dad would miss these moments if given the choice. Probably one of the reasons we don't see her very often.

We usually see Grandma Mutz on all the major holidays, but the Fourth of July is the only get-together she'll host. That's her day to shine.

Lots of people. Lots of food. Lots of explosions.

If you're invited to Grandma Mutz's on the Fourth of July, you're on her exclusive list of people she doesn't hate.

All of her neighbors come (I think they're afraid to tell her no) and bring a side dish that's always scoopable, in a bowl, and frequently involves some form of marshmallow. Very few of them have kids. Only people like Grandma Mutz live on her street. They've lived there for forty years, are bitter toward the world, and have every intention of dying in their home.

We've never seen other kids there, just our parents and Grandma's friends, who've always loved seeing the three grandkids, particularly Sofia. She can do no wrong there. Most adult parties are awful for me, but I've never minded this one. I could always eat as much as I wanted and my hands got to touch more fireworks each passing year.

The driveway is always laid out like a Thanksgiving dinner, just not a fancy one. Three tables form an arc in front of the garage. On the left is the snack table full of chips, vegetables, and crackers. It's an unspoken rule that something has to be dipped to earn property at the snack table. The dessert table is on the opposite side of the driveway: Mom's cookies, Aunt Rose's German chocolate cake, and Grandma Mutz's rhubarb pie. No one likes her pie. Grandma Mutz sees an empty pie pan as a great compliment, and uneaten pie is hugely offensive. There is no middle ground, and everyone always takes a slice knowing this.

The middle table remains empty until it's time to eat. An impressive display of meat prepared by Uncle Mike appears, to complete the triad of food tables. He always takes a moment to admire it before telling everyone it's ready. A sense of pride seems to register as he gazes upon the variety of pork links piled on a platter that requires two hands to carry. He has a tried-and-true method for grilling bratwurst. Turn them only once after finishing a beer. They're ready to serve when the second beer is gone.

The centerpiece of the driveway is a powder-blue wading pool with smiling red crabs on the side. It would be a great place for the kids to play, but there's no room for lounging or splashing on the Fourth. You can't see the bottom of the pool through the layers of Pabst Blue Ribbon, ice, and more PBR. Everything about Grandma Mutz's party is excessive, down to the beer, and the red-white-and-blue cans are a staple of the event. None of the adults ever grab one without tossing at least three to anyone who raises their hand. That year, when I was nine, there were plenty of cans flying around.

"Hey! There he is! Mr. Show!" Uncle Mike shouted while catching a PBR tossed in his general direction. He was skilled enough to do it without even looking. "Now the party can officially begin!"

Woody. Everybody loves Woody. The bachelor of the street, who always brings something extra to a party.

Woody was a pipe fitter with my grandpa for years. Even though my grandpa died a long time ago, Woody still checked in on Grandma Mutz. Anything that needs to be moved, fixed, or taken away, Woody has been there for her. This year, as usual, he walked up the driveway with a paper grocery bag in each arm. The bags were almost as big as he was. He looks like he's my grandma's age, but he's half her size.

All the neighbors sent up a little cheer for Woody's arrival, as did the three of us. We knew what he had in those bags. Grandma actually walked over to greet him, which she didn't even do for her own kids.

"Didn't know if you'd forgotten or blown your hand off." This was "Hello. Nice to see you" for Grandma Mutz.

"Oh, no. Tried a new place today. Was a bit farther past the state line, but they had Dragon's Tears. I wanted those for the finale."

"Oh, Lord, Woody. You and Albert could never get fireworks without spending a day on it. Like when you drove to Cedarbrook, telling me it was the only place you could get whatever it was you were looking for, when you just wanted burgers from Manny's." Grandma Mutz cracked a smile, as she always did when speaking of her husband. "You two looked for trouble anywhere you could find it."

"Hey, wasn't our fault we needed some burgers to wash down the beers!" he cheerfully responded. "Albert was the instigator; I was just the driver. You know that, Mutz."

"Likely story . . . as always."

Woody is one of the few people who could make her smile. This was also one of the rare times I heard about my grandpa. Mom never talks about him, even if I ask. As Woody and Grandma shared stories about her husband, Mom busied herself setting up a vegetable tray.

Woody hadn't even set the bags down before Patrick shoved his head into one like a horse with a feed bag. Woody didn't seem to mind. Anyone excited about fireworks was fine by him.

"Got something for you young fellers, too," he said with a wink. Patrick's head was still in the bag.

"Patrick! Get back and let Woody get a beer before you bug him!" Uncle Mike knew what would happen and probably wanted to delay it. Patrick and fireworks was not a combination anyone imagined would lead to a happy ending. Patrick stepped away from the bag, never taking his eyes off it. This was too much for him. It was almost unfair to tell him he was about to play with fireworks but that he had to wait. You don't put a steak in front of a lion and say, "Now, sit like a good boy." Woody knew this.

"It's all right, Mikey," Woody reassured him. "They can get a look."

No one calls my uncle "Mikey." Woody is allowed to because he's Woody.

"I got something that'll keep these boys busy for a while."

I was done with being polite, too. I was right there with Patrick. I had to know what was in that bag. I did my best to contain my curiosity, but I found my eyes drawn to the packages of gunpowder and light displays.

Woody looked at Sofia, who was in her usual place, standing quietly behind Patrick. "Over here, honey." He motioned for her to stand in front of his chair, with the two bags at his feet. He pulled out a package that resembled a shrunken tissue box with a picture of a mushroom cloud on it. He opened the top and gently pulled out a white ball no bigger than her thumbnail.

"Now, these are for you." He spoke slowly and gestured his hands. Sofia grinned while studying the tiny object.

"Just throw it on the ground. Throw it hard, and watch." He mimicked the motion before handing it to Sofia. She cocked her hand back and hurled the small explosive to the ground to see it ignite into a spark. A few of the women jumped a bit in their seat, not expecting the pop when it hit the ground. Sofia smiled at the sparks she created. She signed "Thank you" and ran to Aunt Rose to show her the gift.

"She sure is getting big, Mikey! Say, how's the . . . ?" He tapped his ear without finishing the question.

"Trying out a new hearing aid next month. Hopefully she'll be good as new once that happens." Uncle Mike and Aunt Rose were always more hopeful than realistic when dealing with Sofia's hearing loss. They never put much effort into learning sign language, and a "hearing aid that should do the trick" was always coming soon.

"Where's mine?" Patrick yelled. He was used to

Sofia being served first, but the wait was killing him. Woody sat in the lawn chair and reached into the bag again. He was our patriotic Santa Claus.

"All right . . . got something for you gents, too."

Using both hands, he pulled out two cheap-looking aprons with the top part missing. One was blue, the other green. He held them up, paused, and looked at us with a serious face.

"Now, boys, in each of these is one hundred of the Chief's finest Tiger Tamers." He put the aprons on his lap and pulled something out of the blue one. It looked like a tiny stick of dynamite.

"Each of these is a little firecracker. Just reach in and grab one, light it, and toss her away." He said this while holding the blue one for me to grab.

He didn't ask which color we wanted. I knew what was coming.

"No! I want the blue one! I get it!" Patrick screamed, reaching toward the apron. Woody is like Grandma Mutz and everyone else on her block: demands shouted by children aren't well received.

"You want one at all?" Woody asked, holding up the green pouch filled with Patrick's treasure. "Or should I give both to Jimmy?" Patrick conceded and reluctantly said thank you. He threw a scornful look my way; he wouldn't be over this anytime soon.

"All right. Last thing." Woody produced a sparkler and lit it, but instead of sparks, it only made a dull light on the end. "This here's a punk. The end stays lit just enough for you to light your wick. Light the Tamer till you see a spark, and toss it quick. If it goes off in your hand, it won't blow it off; it'll just hurt like a bee sting is all."

Bee stings terrify me. I would never say "is all" when referencing a bee sting. He lit the wick, tossed it into the grass, and four seconds later came the pop. There was no color, no big display, just a tiny explosion. It was awesome. Woody lit a punk for each of us and took his seat. "Have fun. I got plenty more when yous run out."

Dad grinned at our excitement. "Why don't you boys head to the back with those? And be sure to thank Mr. Danielson."

Patrick and I each thanked Woody with our shoulders already turned to bolt to the backyard. We raced around the house holding our Olympic torch punks, ready to start the games.

Grandma's backyard is large, oddly shaped, and full of trees. Unlike the front yard, it's never well kept.

Varieties of weeds, overgrown bushes, and thorns that have frequently given us scrapes and rashes scatter the back. This was my chance to take my revenge on the foliage as I lit wick after wick, tossing them into the green. It didn't take much time for Patrick to see how long he could hold one before letting it go. He always managed to toss it just before it went off. I had no interest in locating my pain threshold. I just liked the power of making things go boom.

Patrick and I went through the stock in our pouches and reloaded with Woody twice. Each time, he gladly handed over a new spool of fifty Tiger Tamers and told us to have fun as we ran behind the house. He was one of the best people on earth. I was sure of it.

As we finished our third batch, Mom called for us to eat. We walked to the front, where all the adults were in line, except Uncle Mike. He stood on the opposite side of the meat table, soaking in all the compliments for his culinary skills. He sipped his beer after every word of approval as if toasting himself. Brats and hot dogs didn't seem too hard to make, but Uncle Mike had us convinced he'd completed a masterpiece.

A round card table was set up at the end of the driveway. The kids' table: a term I've grown to despise more and more over the years. My parents have never understood how incredibly awkward the kids' table is for me. Sofia doesn't talk. Patrick wasn't exactly a conversationalist. Not really my ideal seating arrangement.

Sofia took her usual few bites, while Patrick and I sucked back our hot dogs and potato salad as quickly as possible. We didn't even bother taking our pouches off, since we were going back to our fireworks as soon as our plates were cleaned.

It felt a little strange to finish my dinner quickly so I could go play with Patrick. I was actually having fun with him.

Once we were done eating, neither of us bothered asking to be excused. We had work to do. Woody must have known our intentions when we stood up. In one motion, he set his beer next to his chair and handed us the spools. We now had the last fifty Tiger Tamers in our pouches, and they weren't going to blow themselves up.

"Can I have the blue pouch now?" Patrick asked, using his nice voice. I knew he wouldn't let that go.

"No," I responded without looking at him.

"Why?"

"What difference does it make?"

"Exactly. What's the difference?"

"No," I said again, and started walking to another part of the yard. I wanted to enjoy the last explosions. We were about to start our final run of bombings when Patrick said the words that always made me cringe.

"I have an idea."

I knew it was going to involve the fireworks, and unfortunately, I was too curious to ignore his idea this time. I paused to hear the plan.

"Let's save half of these for when it gets dark. That way we can really see the explosions light up."

All right . . . actually not a horrible idea. I kind of did want to see those explosions at night. He could tell I was mulling it over and chimed in again with more details.

"Take half and put them on the step. We'll come back when it's dark so we can see them light up." I agreed, and we made two piles on the back step and fired off what remained in our pouches before heading to the front of the house.

"Ten minutes till showtime!" Woody called out to us while tying the extended wick to what he called the finale. The end of the driveway held the remaining contents of the two paper bags. Each firework was perfectly spaced from the next and had a label that offered a hint of that device's personality. At the end of the line stood what resembled a small cannon. Woody always uses one long wick to connect all the fireworks. His goal is to light the far end and sit back for the show. He has never disappointed.

Mom and Aunt Rose were helping to put food away while Dad moved the grill. Sofia stood by her parents, twirling a green sparkler to cast spells in the air. Apparently, Woody had a few more gifts for her than he had let on. Uncle Mike was telling the guys his "camping in the rain" story (a story that always makes an appearance at parties), and I could see the color showing in his cheeks. Not an embarrassed shade of red, more of a "twelve pack into the party" red.

Patrick grabbed my arm. "Ten minutes — let's go!"

He was right. We had ten minutes to see our own nighttime display of tiny explosions. We grabbed our punks and ran to the back. Each of us filled our pouches with the fireworks we'd saved on the back porch. I was thinking about telling Patrick what a good idea this was and giving him a rare compliment. Then he spoke and changed my mind.

"Now can I have the blue one?"

He still wasn't over it. I sensed he wouldn't enjoy
this as much without the blue pouch, but I didn't care. I
didn't get many wins over Patrick and was enjoying this
one, especially since he wouldn't let it go. I didn't even
respond, just took my Tamers and headed toward the
edge of the yard.

I'm not sure what I thought would happen to the
Tiger Tamers in the dark, but it wasn't the impressive
display I'd expected. Really not much more than it was
in the light. Either way, they still went boom and that
was enough for me. With twenty left now, I was going
to make them count.

"Whoa! Check this out!" Patrick yelled from the
far corner of the yard. Whenever Patrick said "Check
this out," it meant he'd found an animal, a dead animal,
or something he could use as a weapon. "This thing is
so fat!"

Animal.

Crouched on his heels, he was holding a stick and
prodding the largest toad I had ever seen.

"Look how fat he is! I bet he can't even jump."
He poked it again. The toad hopped its front end in

a semicircle, turning away from Patrick. "He's so fat! Come on, boy. I bet you can jump farther than that," he said while poking it from underneath. "Hey, I know what will make you jump. . . ."

Oh, no.

Patrick stood up and reached into his pouch to retrieve a Tamer. Before I could say anything, he had it lit and tossed it in the direction of the toad. Three seconds later, the explosion that must have been massive to the small creature forced it to hop its body away from the noise. Only two hops, though. I so wished it could scurry or fly or do something else animals do to get away. It just sat there. This was only going to get worse.

"Hmmm. Let's try that again. I bet we can get him to jump higher." He reached for another.

"Wait . . . you're gonna hurt it." I knew my words wouldn't matter. The toad looked straight ahead, and I swear it had tears in its eyes. I knew amphibians don't cry, but this one was crying. Patrick had already thrown another Tamer, this time behind it. It hopped twice and was now closer to Patrick. It had no idea what was coming.

"Let's see if we can make it hop straight up," he said with one hand on a new Tamer.

"You're going to hurt it. Just let it go." The toad looked directly at me with its tear-filled eyes, asking for help.

Another explosion.

"Let's set one on top of it. Wonder if it'll blow up." He already had the next Tamer lit. In my head flashed an image of this animal's guts on my shoes. I grabbed his arm as he reached toward the toad.

"No! Just leave it alone!"

Too late.

The Tamer exploded.

The toad was fine, but Patrick howled in pain. The Tamer was in his hand when it blew. Woody was right. He didn't lose any fingers; it just hurt like a bee sting.

He gripped his wounded hand while staring at his fingers, probably to make sure everything was still attached. Once he realized nothing had blown off, he shoved me to the ground. "That hurt!"

I propped myself up on my elbows and was about to explain when I realized what was coming.

"Let's see how you like it."

He had already tossed a lit Tamer. It landed on my shirt. I screamed. I shook it off to see it fall just before exploding. He already had another in his hand.

"Patrick, stop it!" I made it to my feet before the next Tamer went off in front of me. Since Patrick had spent a good part of the afternoon timing his throws, he was pretty good at tossing them before they burst.

"Stop it!" I ran toward the front. Another explosion at my heels. "Patrick, stop!" I turned when I reached the side of the house to see he had thrown one at my arm. It bounced off and popped midair. I cried out for help. I needed an adult to hear me.

When I reached the front yard, I searched for my parents without breaking stride. I couldn't help but notice the Roman candle spraying the sidewalk with pink sparks. Woody's show had begun. Everyone had moved their chairs up against the house. My feet turned and darted back toward the crowd.

"STOP!"

I wanted everyone to hear me. I wanted Patrick to be in trouble.

He was so caught up in getting me back, he hadn't noticed all the adults watching us. He threw his last Tamer, perfectly timed to explode on my neck.

The light tap of the undetonated firecracker would have left a slight itch had it not exploded, but I heard the wick simmer and knew I was doomed. I couldn't see the actual explosion, but sure felt it. Bee stings don't hurt nearly as bad as that tiny stick of dynamite did.

The adults now had two shows to watch. Woody's fireworks display at the end of the driveway and Patrick torturing me in the middle. I turned toward the house, clutching my neck to see four figures leap from their chairs. My parents and Patrick's.

Mom's eyes widened. Her chair fell over as she darted toward me, saying something I couldn't hear. Dad got to me first. He took my head and positioned my face toward him. He must have thought it was my eye. Uncle Mike dropped his beer and made his way for Patrick. Aunt Rose shot up with the same look of fear Mom had. But she wasn't looking at me. Or Patrick.

She was looking at her husband.

Six steps later, he had Patrick by the arm that was holding the lit punk. "What is your problem? You stupid? That it?" His grip tightened on Patrick. Aunt Rose had her hands on my uncle's other arm as he glared down at his son. "You could have blasted his eye out! I asked you a question! Are you stupid?" His words came out in a flurry of syllables as if they were just one long word. A long, angry word.

"He's fine, Mike. No harm, just shaken." Concern filled my dad's voice, but it wasn't for me any longer. Aunt Rose was stroking my uncle's arm as if he were the one injured.

A blast of red light flashed from above, matched with a thunderous boom. The finale.

"ANSWER ME!"

Patrick cowered, then stuttered the word "sorry" over and over.

"Are you stupid?"

Uncle Mike broke away from Aunt Rose's grip and had Patrick by both shoulders. He forgot Patrick was still holding the lit punk. While only a small source of heat, anyone would feel it pressed against their skin. Uncle Mike felt it.

"Ouch! What the —?" He reactively pushed Patrick away and grabbed his burned forearm. Patrick hit the pavement and howled.

"Sorry! Sorry! I'm sorry!"

"It's fine, Mike. Enough." Two bursts of purple went off and nearly drowned out Grandma Mutz's commands while she stood with her hands on the shoulders of a terrified Sofia.

Whether the noise of the finale was too much or Uncle Mike was too drunk, he ignored her completely. The way he stood over Patrick reminded me of a picture I saw of Muhammad Ali standing over his opponent after a knockout.

"Get up and stop crying!"

The finale must have been reaching its climax. A rapid-fire series of light bursts put Uncle Mike and Patrick into a silhouette against a backdrop of color and noise.

Uncle Mike reached down and grabbed Patrick's wrist. He yanked him up the same way he starts his lawn mower. Patrick came up. And immediately went back down.

"My arm! Ow! My arm!" Patrick rolled on his back, clutching his elbow. His legs kicked at the air in this wild and out-of-control way. "My arm! Oh, God, it hurts! Please!"

I couldn't move. I couldn't watch.

I didn't want this.

"Get up, you baby," Uncle Mike said, like this was common, as if Patrick didn't get the toy he wanted. "Get up."

"Mike, I think he's hurt," Dad said, moving toward Patrick.

"He's fine. He does this. Now, get up!"

"Mike, his arm. I think it's bro —"

"Think I don't know what a broken arm looks like? He's fine."

I didn't know what I wanted to see happen. I knew Patrick was hurt. I knew I didn't want to see Uncle Mike pick him up.

Before anyone else could react, Uncle Mike grabbed Patrick and threw him over his shoulder the way a fireman carries someone from a burning house. He tossed his son into a lawn chair. Patrick howled and pleaded. It didn't do any good.

The popping of the finale had stopped, and the driveway was left with smoldering wisps of smoke and whimpers.

Uncle Mike had his hands on the arms of the chair and crouched down to face Patrick. "You're fine. Stop crying. You're ruining the party."

Patrick bit his lip and clutched his arm. He winced, tears streaming down his cheeks. Aunt Rose was now stroking my uncle's back. Patrick took a breath. The kind that comes before someone lets out a wailing cry.

Uncle Mike's knuckles turned white as he clenched the chair. "I said —"

"Mikey —"

Uncle Mike turned.

He let go of the chair. He had to; otherwise he wouldn't have caught the beer Woody tossed at him. Uncle Mike never missed a tossed beer.

"Kids cry, Mikey. It's all right. You having a beer with me or what?"

Another beer was the absolute last thing he needed, but Woody did that for Patrick, not my uncle. Uncle Mike walked away from Patrick, muttering something about how whiny kids get, and apologized to Woody for his son ruining the fireworks.

Aunt Rose took Patrick inside, where Sofia brought him ice and let him cry. I stayed outside with my parents as Uncle Mike had a few more beers and laughs with Woody. He kept telling Woody how sorry he was about Patrick: how they didn't know what to do with him because he had no self-control. I don't know why we stayed when none of us wanted to be there.

I didn't want to see Patrick crying inside. I didn't want to be around Uncle Mike outside. I stayed close to my parents and pretended to help them clean up.

Uncle Mike was loud again, telling Woody how Patrick needed discipline. Mom turned toward Uncle Mike, stared right through him. Then she stepped toward him.

Oh, no. She was going to yell at him for how he treated Patrick. But she didn't get more than two steps before being stopped. Her wrist was anchored by her mother's viselike grip.

"Don't interfere."

Mom was still locked on Uncle Mike as he took another sip. Her shoulders were aimed to confront him, even with Grandma Mutz holding her wrist.

"Not your family. Don't interfere," she repeated until Mom relaxed. Still in her lawn chair, Grandma Mutz stopped her daughter from creating more fireworks.

Every time we see my grandma, I learn more family rules.

The next July I asked if we were going to Grandma's again. Mom told me she wasn't having the party that year. When I asked why, she just said, "The neighborhood wants to keep things quieter is all."

I didn't believe that.

I felt terrible about that night, about when Patrick was hurt. I hoped his arm wasn't broken and was relieved to hear it wasn't. His father had only dislocated his elbow when he yanked him off the driveway.

The doctor told Patrick he was lucky because it healed faster than a break. And things would be back to normal any day.

I didn't believe that, either.

*CHAPTER 4

Everyone has a breaking point.

The back room of Wainwright's Funeral Home. My Fortress of Solitude. A sanctuary of stale sugar cookies and watered-down red punch, with no one around to bother me. It'll do just fine for now.

OK, deep breath. This is what happens in movies when people are stuck, physically or otherwise. They take a breath, focus, and a solution presents itself.

Here goes.

Inhale. Deep bre —

Oh, no.

I feel it. As small as it is, no doubt in my mind that's a thread popping with relief. The button won't last. A belt could have totally saved me. But of course this is the day I can't find it. It's not like I have a bunch of extra belts lying around for all my fancy pants.

OK, maybe just small breaths. Maybe small breaths will get me to where I need to be. Just sip some air and let tomorrow's words find me.

Small breath . . . Patrick —

Small breath . . . was —

Small breath . . . Patrick was —

Small breath . . .

Useless. There's no way I'll be able to think of something nice to say by morning.

I hate this so much. Why can't Patrick's parents be the ones to talk about him? Even when he's dead, I still lose to him.

At least it's quieter in here. I know this is borrowed time, and any second a new awkward person will come through the entryway with more questions I can't answer.

A pile of over-energized kids rushes in from the hall, storming my castle. The stale cookies won't know what hit them. Time to go.

I get back to the entrance of the main parlor only to

see that it's even more crowded than before. Mom and Aunt Rose are still at the front door greeting people.

A lanky older man arrives. Mom greets him first with a hug and smile. Her arms turn slightly toward her sister to subtly guide the man to her. In perfect sync, Aunt Rose reciprocates by turning her torso to the guest being passed her way. They don't look at each other through the exchange. Each half of the twin knows what the other will do. A silent communication flows between them as guests interact with the sisters. As much as their parasitic relationship bothers me, I have to admit it's impressive at times.

"Oh. Oh, my. Girls, it has been too long," a large woman boasts to Mom and my aunt.

Mrs. Whitehead walks through the entryway. In grade school she always ran the spring carnival. And the Halloween fest. And the book drive. She liked being in charge. I don't know when the last of her kids went through the school, but no one had the guts to tell her she couldn't be in charge of social functions anymore. She's a beastly woman with gorilla-like man hands. Maybe those hands intimidated people and they were too afraid of them to say no.

Mrs. Whitehead hugs Mom first. As much as she

tries, Mom can't hide her discomfort of being in the warm embrace of this woman. Aunt Rose is next. She gets a similar hug with an added bonus: Mrs. Whitehead grips my aunt's wrists as she comes out of the hug, almost like she's afraid to let go. Aunt Rose grimaces, as she is probably losing circulation in her fingertips. I take a sick pleasure in this. She deserves a little pain for sacrificing me to the podium tomorrow.

Mrs. Whitehead finally releases her. Mostly. She lets one of Aunt Rose's wrists go and slides the other gorilla club down to my aunt's hand. Mrs. Whitehead smiles while pulling my aunt toward the other side of the room, making it clear she wants to show her something. It reminds me of the way our neighbor wanted to show off his new car. Aunt Rose doesn't even need to look at Mom; she knows to follow and help her sister.

I remember in science when we talked about diffusion. We did this lab with carrots and water. Each of us got two carrots. One went in a beaker of water, the other in a beaker with nothing. We let the carrots sit overnight and examined them the next day. We had to answer the question "Where did the water go?" The carrot sitting in water was crisp, and crunchy (Hannah Verlander ate it against protocol), and full of water. The other was dry, soft, and bendable. The water molecules went where they found space. Whether that was in the carrot or in the air, they moved to open space.

By the law of diffusion, I'll continue to go where there's space. Thank you, Mrs. Whitehead, for creating space for me.

I creep my way to the newly minted clearing, hoping no one grabs me. The open space won't last, but I'll take any victory right now.

This wall is perfect to lean against for the remainder of my time here. I'll have a few moments befor —

Something winks at me from the floor. Something shiny.

It can't be.

I've never seen it in the open like this.

It sparkles against the dull beige carpet, almost calling out to me.

Aunt Rose's beetle bracelet.

It actually isn't a beetle, but a weevil, or at least that's what Aunt Rose says. The story goes that their father gave the girls their own silver bracelets for high-school graduation. On each was a charm of something in nature that wants to be around the flowers they were named after. Lily got a butterfly, Rose a weevil. I think it's a beetle and he just told her it was a rose weevil because it sounds more poetic, but she firmly believes that her hot-tempered, alcoholic father scoured the earth to find an abstract insect charm just for her.

Mom and her sister have an undeniable bond, but this is one area they differ.

Aunt Rose never took her bracelet off; Mom never put hers on. I asked her about it once. It went on my list of questions that are quickly dismissed. The same happens when I ask anything about my grandfather. Grandma Mutz will sing like a canary about him, but Mom locks up and moves on. I even asked where her bracelet is and only got "in a safe place."

The rose weevil bracelet, however, is as much a part of my aunt as her own thumb. She is never without it and would be devastated if it were ever lost. It's like her Achilles' heel. Except, she's not really that strong to start with. And she cries over anything. Still, it's one of her weaknesses.

It must have fallen off when Mrs. Whitehead held on with her mighty ogre-like hello. This is so surreal, to see it somewhere other than on Aunt Rose's wrist. I've seen her without her wedding ring but never without her bracelet. Her emotional throttle will go off the

105

charts if she thinks it's lost. I should get it back to her before a disaster happens.

I should get it to her now.

I really should.

Or . . .

You know what?

Let her come unhinged.

She wants me to step up to a mic tomorrow and make things up about a person who has tortured me all my life while she sits quietly in a pew, judging what I say. She wants to set me up for failure by putting me on display for all the world to see because she's too scared to do it herself.

No.

No, I should help.

I should.

Besides, if she doesn't find her bracelet, she'll drag Mom into her mess. Then Mom will be upset because her sister is upset because Aunt Rose could never just be upset by herself. Then Mom would be an anxious mess trying to calm Aunt Rose down.

Mom . . .

The one who told me I was doing this speech for Aunt Rose no matter what. The one who thinks I can perform like a circus monkey and doesn't want to hear anything else from me. The one who smacked me down when I told her I didn't want to do it.

Actually, if Aunt Rose lost her bracelet . . .

I shouldn't interfere.

I move strategically from the wall and stand in the center of my newfound space. The silver beetle is securely out of sight, resting in the crevice between the front of my heel and forefoot. I don't want to break it — I just want to watch someone besides me experience panic for a moment.

With hands in pockets and my best casual face on, I look toward my aunt to see if she's noticed. Nothing yet. Mrs. Whitehead still owns her hand and is going over some of the pictures. There must have been one from a school event that caught her eye from across the room. Mom is trying to break the bond without physical contact, but she may be out of options.

Mom's finger points toward the crowd while she looks to be explaining something. I'm sure she's telling Mrs. Whitehead they're needed somewhere. Mom does the shoulder touch on the Yeti and it seems to work. Aunt Rose gets her limb back and forces a smile to Mrs. Whitehead while trying to discreetly rub life back into her hand. Aunt Rose's eyes dart to the side, seeing a horrible image only for her. She looks to her wrist, at the curveball she can't hit.

Showtime.

Aunt Rose's left hand, naked wrist and all, grabs Mom's forearm. She tries to whisper to Mom what happened, but her emotions won't allow a quiet voice. In the same way they greeted and passed guests, the twins work as a team, with all four eyes in perfect synchronization, darting on the ground below them.

Still clutching Mom, Aunt Rose murmurs something to herself. Their shoulders tense upward together. Both necks crane higher, almost as if they're trying to float so they don't disturb the crime scene. Their eyes work as a unit, and I watch the desperation set in. I envision an imaginary improv teacher instructing them, "You're on a rickety ship, and if you move too much, you sink. Go!" Aunt Rose's face crinkles, Mom's is frantic, confused.

Good.

Now they know what it feels like.

Any second now, they're going to retrace their steps and head my way. I won't be able to pretend I didn't know I was stepping on it.

With my eyes forward, I pivot off my heel and slide the guilty foot slightly back. Not too far, just enough where a quick swing of my toe will knock it to the wall and leave me clean.

Casual look, hands still in pockets, three-two-one, swipe . . . and success. I turn on my heels in the direction of the bracelet to see it resting perfectly against the trim. Not too hidden, not too hard to find. I'll let Mom and Aunt Rose stew for a bit more. If they still can't figure out it was Professor Plum with the wrench in the library, then I'll act like I found it and tell—

Sofia?

How long was she standing there?

Did she see me kick the bracelet? I swear that girl is part cat.

I give her a wave, trying to not look like I just performed an incredibly cruel act against her mom. She nibbles on the remains of a back-room cookie. She must have ducked in there after I left. She waves back with her Norman hand. I can't read her face.

I'm turning. Yup. It's happening. I'm Hulking out. But instead of going green and gaining strength, I go red and sweaty. Maybe she didn't see. Maybe she just got there. Maybe I'm overreacting.

Wait. Aunt Rose and Mom aren't retracing their steps? I thought for sure they'd come over here and see it and this would be done. Where are they going? Oh, no. She's going to get Uncle Mike.

She's going to cry to him and he's going to get overwhelmed. And angry.

Then Mom will tell Dad to defuse the situation.

Then he'll get overwhelmed. And frustrated.

That's how it always goes.

Aunt Rose makes it to her husband. He and Dad are standing by Patrick's casket. Her hands are no longer under control as she explains what happened and gives my uncle the task of "Just fix it somehow." The familiar look of submission takes over his face. Mom talks to Dad but in a more controlled manner. It isn't his fight, but he's in it now.

It wasn't supposed to happen this way.

All four of them start talking at once. The couple in line takes a step back. I can see their indecisiveness; they aren't sure if they should continue to wait or just move straight to the casket.

Guilt churns from deep in my stomach. It wasn't supposed to be like this. I just . . . I don't even know. I need to walk away. I need to not be here right now. I'm red and sweaty and can't breathe and want new pants and to not be here and —

"Oh! Thank you, sweetie! Thank you!" shouts an exuberant Aunt Rose.

Aunt Rose gives her daughter a tight hug while the husbands exhale that the crisis is over. Before the chaos hit the masses, before the imaginary ship sank, the bracelet found its owner.

Sofia. Without anyone seeing her assassin-like movements, she scooped up the lost treasure and returned it to the rightful owner.

Did she see me after all? She doesn't miss much.

My face likely has traces of guilt, and I decide to stay put and out of their way. Sofia holds her mom's hand as the sisters return to their post at the entrance. The husbands get the line moving again. All seems right in this world of wakes and funerals as if the last four minutes never happened.

I didn't do anything wrong, though. Right? I'm not the one who knocked it off her wrist. I didn't totally hide it. I didn't initiate anything. I shouldn't even feel bad. I just . . . let things happen.

Why didn't I see it playing out this way? Aunt Rose is always the first domino to fall, followed by Mom,

Uncle Mike, then Dad. Patrick was the one who always started this chain reaction.

Now I'm the one who created the chaos.

Maybe I'm no better than Patrick.

Aunt Rose always thought if Patrick had a creative outlet, he could get himself under control. Sports were usually out, because they require teamwork (a lesson learned in soccer when he head-butted a girl in our first-grade league), and so was anything dealing with art (as that involved Patrick sitting still, which was nearly impossible). Aunt Rose mentioned Scouts once. Uncle Mike kept eyes on her while he turned his head to the left, and mouthed, "Knives?" then to the right, "Fire?" She nodded in compliance.

When the flyer came home with all third-graders for a nonathletic, noncompetitive club, hope was renewed for Patrick to find a calling.

And so, the common theme of my childhood appeared again in the form of Young Engineers Club: another organized group, run by volunteers, that would be "really good for Patrick."

Patrick seemed genuinely excited for it, though. If he joined, that meant Mom would make sure I was soon to follow. I actually was kind of interested, too. I just wished my parents would have asked me instead of telling me.

We met every Thursday night for two hours at Monroe Grade School. Each session had a routine: the volunteers gave us a set of materials and a building task. The first week's challenge was to construct a bridge that could hold a one-pound weight; the next week it was a working pulley that could lift the same weight. Since the group was open to anyone in grades three through six, the older kids typically could complete the task while the younger kids struggled not to spill glue.

Patrick actually did all right there. He was a little riled up at first, but once we'd get our task, he managed fine. The difference between Young Engineers and every other group Aunt Rose threw him into was this club didn't follow the cardinal rule of youth organizations: cooperation was *not* required. As each task was unveiled, we could work with whomever we wanted, or alone. Patrick and I worked parallel to each other — but not necessarily together. For once, it worked. Patrick still hung the imaginary "__ days since last incident" sign around his neck, but so far this group didn't entice his episodes by forcing him to work with others.

However, that counter went back to zero when we had the pinnacle of every Young Engineer's experience: the YE Glider Launch.

It was mentioned at each of our previous meetings. The buzz from the older kids spoke for itself that this was the biggest night for Young Engineers.

All Young Engineers, regardless of age, were equal in the eyes of the Launch. The winners could be from any group. It was all about which glider flew the farthest. Trophies were awarded for first-, second-, and third-longest flights, plus one for most creative design.

When the night arrived, Patrick confidently strolled in with his dad, armed with a paper bag of supplies.

"Hey, Jimmy! You ready to see me win?" he exclaimed with a just-struck-it-rich grin while setting his bag down as if it were the first-place trophy.

"Sure. But I doubt that's going to happen," I responded, scanning the older groups with their toolboxes and various contraptions ready for their gliders. Having been here before, they clearly had an advantage on what would work. "I think these guys know what they're doing better than us."

"They don't know what I've got in mind," he said, looking at his prized paper bag. His eyes were alive, a look I knew well. It was the look that meant he'd been cooking something big in his brain. Sometimes this was a bad thing, but if he got fixated on something creative, it could be pretty cool. I could tell he'd mapped something out. Whatever he was planning to do with his glider, it got me curious.

The rules of the night were simple. Every Engineer was given a kit with the exact same components. Each box contained:

1 cylinder of wood for the body

1 set of wings

2 nails for the wings

We had one hour of work time to meet the specifications required. It had to weigh at least three ounces, fit in the confines of the measuring box, and use all the kit materials. You could also bring extra components, paint, or whatever you wanted. Besides the dimensions, anything was fair game to create a glider that could outfly the rest.

One more rule echoed through our ears that every participant was told to follow. A rule that required the honor system, which was the core of what it meant to be a Young Engineer:

Thou shalt not have thy parents build for thee.

When the volunteer mom passed out the kits, she was very direct that it should be our project and not our parents' work.

"All right, Young Engineers! Listen up!" the head parent announced. "Before we get started, here's what your task is for the Glider Launch. Next to me is an example of simple engineering I created myself for tonight." He stood next to a small machine sitting on a cart. His pudgy hand rested proudly on it. I pictured his son in place of the device.

"This here is our launchpad. Built her myself with some basic knowledge of engineering. Started with a tennis-ball shooter and made some changes for our needs. Now we have a fully functioning glider launcher of our own." His free hand rose, awaiting applause. While enjoying his reception, "I should start selling these on the side" was casually conveyed to another dad on his left.

"Here's how it works. I turn it on, set your glider in, and we watch her fly." The proud creator of the launcher placed a wood cylinder from a kit into the machine. He gave it a nudge and we watched as the shape took to the air.

"And yours truly," he boasted, hand on his heart, "will be your Launch Coordinator for the evening." His hand raised, again, for applause.

"All right, Young Engineers, you have one hour. The clock starts"—he paused, soaking in the power of his moment—"now!"

Kits ripped open, tools clamored, and voices fell quiet as the Young Engineers dove into their work.

I felt pretty good about my idea. I knew the stealth bomber was one of the fastest planes, so I decided to mimic that design. I dumped my bag of scissors, black paint, and a few other additions that I thought would give me a fighting chance, and got to work.

First the paint. I was smart enough to know it'd need time to dry. I could work on the other parts while that happened. I laid out the hammer and nails, ready to use them while the paint dried.

"Perfect. Yes," Patrick said to himself while his scissors meticulously cut away at a sheet of sticker paper.

A couple of finished shapes were already on the table. I had no idea what they were, but they seemed to make sense to him. His supply bag was turned on its side, empty. Besides the sticker paper, all he had was a key chain with a little ghost attached. He wasn't doing anything to the structure of the glider, only decorating it. He didn't stand a chance. Not my problem. I continued to focus on my own work while monitoring the clock.

With my paint now dry, I could fashion the wings to look like a stealth bomber. Ten minutes left: plenty of time to attach them and add some weight to the front for an extra boost. Patrick could waste all the time he wanted on decorations; mine would soar.

"Time! Everyone to the launcher!" announced the proud owner of the launching machine. "Ladies and gentlemen, let's fly some gliders!" This guy really loved tonight.

My stealth bomber sat in front of me, facing Patrick's mess of white stickers on wings. I was pretty happy with my work, until it sat across from Patrick's. Now I loved it. Various zigs and zags cluttered his wings in no recognizable pattern. The little ghost was off the key chain and glued clumsily to the top. He deserved whatever ridicule was coming his way.

"Third-graders! Form a line behind me!" the Launch Coordinator commanded. We hurried into a clustered line with our creations at the ready.

The launchpad claimed the far end of the gym. One of the volunteer dads stood ready in the flight path with masking tape. He'd write the Young Engineer's name on a piece, then mark the spot where their glider hit the floor.

Two boys were ahead of me. The first launch of the night was a success for a fleeting moment before the wings separated from the body. A failure. He took it well though. The second glider flew no better but did manage to keep the wings intact a little longer.

My turn. I no longer wanted to win as much as not be embarrassed by having it fall apart. I handed over my product, careful to not drop it in the exchange. It rested in the launchpad, awaiting the nudge from the Launch Coordinator. With my jaw clenched, I watched my stealth bomber take to the air and stay afloat for a respectable distance.

A hand patted my shoulder as my landing was marked. "All right! Looks like you're the man to beat so far! Great flight!"

I was in the lead. Only two other kids had gone, but I

was winning for a moment and it felt amazing. Applause for my flight followed the Launch Coordinator's comments. I got why he liked his role so much.

By the time the rest of my age group went, I was a distant fourth. The girl next in line outsailed my glider by several feet, as did the two other boys. Still, mine had worked, and that was a victory.

Only one third-grader remained in line: Patrick. He'd never waited to be the last person in a line. This was new.

Patrick handed his mess of a glider over to be placed in the launcher. As soon as it left his hands, he stopped the room.

"Wait!" Patrick exclaimed with his arms extended like a traffic cop. "Turn off the lights!"

"What?" the Launch Coordinator asked. "We can't. We won't be able to see where it lands."

"Yes, you will! I promise! Please?"

Patrick said please? What was he up to? He must have been thinking about this all week. The Launch Coordinator paused for a moment, moved his jaw around, and showed empathy to the boy asking for a special privilege.

"All right, but if we can't spot the landing, that's it. No second chance."

He didn't finish his sentence before Patrick was running to the light switch.

"Three-two-one, go!" he yelled in dramatic fashion while all light left the gym. It would've been completely dark if not for the glow coming from Patrick's glider.

"Welcome to Area 51!" he shouted. None of us could see him, but his voice told us he was smiling big. This was the moment he'd seen in his head for a week.

The ordinary paper he'd surgically cut and pasted to his glider was glow-in-the-dark material. He didn't just slap it on the wings; it made a design that was Patrick's take on alien language. The little ghost he put on top also showed bright on the wings. The murmurs of "Cool!" "Wow!" and "Awesome!" came from the Young Engineers waiting their turn. In the light, it was a mess of a glider. In the dark, it impressed everyone.

"Very nice!" the Launch Coordinator announced. "Now let's see how she flies! Ready and . . . go!"

Patrick's glider took to the air with our eyes tracking the only light in the room. Without the other markers visible, none of us could really tell how successful the flight was. When it did make contact with the ground, the tiny pilot was thrown from the craft. I heard Patrick's footsteps clamoring toward his creation as the lights returned.

The volunteer marking distance was on one knee setting the tape with Patrick's name. While the look was impressive, the flight distance was not. Four pieces of tape were well ahead of Patrick's, including mine. Patrick's dream of victory was over.

That didn't diminish his smile. Patrick picked up his craft and marched it back to our table.

"Sorry, man," I said, offering condolences. "Good try, but I think your pilot hurt your flight. Too heavy."

He smiled even bigger.

"Uh, you didn't even beat mine," I said, in case he needed reminding that mine was better.

"I know."

"Looks like you won't win the trophy," I replied, with his overconfident claim still in my head.

"That wasn't the prize I was trying for."

It took me a second, but then I got it. Patrick knew he would never make a glider that could beat the kids with three years of experience. So did I, but part of me hoped there was a miracle chance. Patrick was smarter.

He'd put all his eggs in the creativity prize basket. And he nailed it. Jealousy turned my attention back to the launch without a response.

For the next few minutes, we watched the older groups take their turns. As expected, the distance of the gliders increased with age and experience. A couple of girls had a commanding lead with their tape markers, but none came close to the showmanship of my cousin.

Finally, it was the sixth-graders' turn. As expected, the first glider from the group soared past all other markers. Three years of experience counted for something. Eight more in the oldest group still had a chance to beat him, though.

The next sixth-grader hurriedly made his way to the launcher. In his excitement, he misread the hand-off to the Launch Coordinator. We witnessed a crash before takeoff, as his glider lay at his feet, wounded with a broken wing. Even though he was one of the oldest kids there, it didn't stop the gush of public tears. His father, the Launch Coordinator, quickly came to his aid, consoling his son and scooping up the lost bird. The Young Engineer, fragile as his blue-and-white glider, sobbed while his dad led him back to their table.

"Hal, hey, let someone else go, and we'll try and

salvage this," he announced to the man with marking tape. One of the moms stepped up to the launcher for the next flight, while the Launch Coordinator produced a screwdriver and tape to save the glider. His son was howling and inconsolable. I could tell it wasn't the first time the father and son had been here.

The remaining gliders took flight, and the top prizes were clear. After the final marking hit the floor, the dad of the broken glider returned.

"Got it! All set!" he announced while leading his son to the launcher. The boy's eye sockets were stained red as he halfheartedly joined his dad. His glider did make it to the launcher this time, but only flew about half as far as the others in his group. His dad's positive pat on the shoulder only jump-started more tears.

"All right, everyone! Fantastic job to all the Young Engineers tonight!" he announced cheerfully, despite his sobbing sidekick. "If everyone could clean up the stations, tape, and anything else while the leaders confer, that would be great. Trophies will be handed out as soon as the gym looks ready."

The Young Engineers took to task but with no sense of urgency. We all knew who the winners were. The two girls and boy with the farthest tape markers took their time picking them up while admiring their achievement. Their parents, shaking hands of congratulations, stood directly behind them.

One Young Engineer moved with energy, though. Patrick. He was about to get the first award of his life. He was smiling with his whole face while cleaning up, waiting for his moment. I was still mad that he had done something smarter than me.

A few minutes later, the floor was free of tape, the tables cleaned, and only the launching machine showed any evidence that the Young Engineers were there. The Engineers stood huddled in grade-level groups, their parents behind them. Dad and Uncle Mike waited behind our station. My uncle looked different from how he had looked at the other YE nights. He looked almost relaxed. He even smiled while watching Patrick clean up his station.

"All right, Young Engineers! You all did a fine job tonight and I'm proud to say we have a new flight record for the Glider Launch! Give yourselves a round of applause for another great year!" the Launch Coordinator proudly bellowed. The Engineers and parents all clapped in a show of sportsmanship for one another. Even though his son was the crier, this guy hadn't stopped smiling through his unshaven face.

"Now, we've got a few trophies to give out before we leave, so let's get to it. Before the top three flights are awarded, let's recognize the creative part of tonight."

Patrick stood taller.

"Part of being a Young Engineer is using your creativity. I was so impressed by all that I saw in this room tonight. You all deserve to be recognized. Really, really impressive," he announced while surveying the room. "But one of you will take home the trophy for most creative."

Another dad moved in on cue, handing him the trophy.

"And most creative goes to . . ."

Patrick rocked on his toes.

"Owen Grumbles and his police plane!"

Applause.

Not for Patrick.

For Owen Grumbles, the Engineer who cried for ten minutes after dropping his glider.

For Owen Grumbles, who graciously accepted the award for most creative glider, a police plane.

126

Owen Grumbles accepted the award for most creative glider from the presenter, Launch Coordinator, and leader of the Young Engineers, Mr. Grumbles.

"What?" Patrick said, drawing stares from those nearby. Uncle Mike nudged him with a flick of his elbow. Patrick only got louder. "Seriously?"

"No," Uncle Mike responded, shifting his weight.

"No? Dad . . . I . . ." Uncle Mike gave him the "Lock it up" stare. "But . . . I can't —"

"Patrick, we need to be good spor —"

"A freakin' police plane? A police plane is the most creative glider here? No!"

Here we go.

The Young Engineers were about to get an education.

"I watched his dad fix it! He cheated!" The words poured out uncontrollably now. "Those were the rules! He cheated! We couldn't have parents help us, and his dad fixed it right in front of us!"

He had a point.

"Patrick, that's enough. There's nothing —"

"His dad fixed it right in front of everyone. And he's his dad! He's seriously giving the award to his own son?"

Episode or not, that's two points for Patrick.

"Enough. We're leaving," Uncle Mike said through his teeth while grabbing Patrick's arm.

"And a police plane? A police plane? That's the most creative glider here? That's more creative than my Area 51 alien craft?"

That was three points for Patrick that no one could argue with. I stepped back to clear the path to the exit Uncle Mike was leading him toward. They made it a few steps until Patrick stopped in front of me.

"Look at Jimmy's glider! His stealth bomber is more creative than the 'police plane'! At least he should have won!" Patrick yelled as he snatched my glider from my hands.

No.

No. I worked too hard on this.

"At least Jimmy painted his himself! I bet that kid's dad painted it for him, too!"

"Patrick, give it back!" I yell just as loud, knowing the fate of my glider when held captive in his hands.

"It's not fair! Jimmy should've won, too! We didn't get help from our parents!"

Uncle Mike had a hand on each of his son's arms. He wasn't completely lifting Patrick off the ground, but Patrick's heels no longer touched the floor.

"Give it back. Now." A hand was on my shoulder — my dad's. I didn't realize I'd moved a step toward the episode. This was new for me. I usually stayed away from the storm when I saw it coming. Not this time. I worked too hard on my glider. I wanted it back.

"Jimmy, let it go," he said, like I was the problem here. I wasn't. I wanted my glider back.

"Give it back. Now!" I said for everyone to hear.

"But it's not fair! It's not!" Patrick said to the audience of open mouths watching the show.

That was it. I didn't care what happened.

"I want my glider back! You break everything! Give it back!" I rejected my father's cue to stand down and grabbed my glider. Dad quickly followed with both hands on my shoulders. I had a grasp on my glider now. I knew it wouldn't survive, but at least I'd have tried to save it.

Until now, I had let Patrick have his episodes and always had to be the bigger person, stepping aside from his path of destruction.

Not tonight. I was going down with the ship.

"Let go of it NOW!" I yelled for every person in the room to hear, especially my dad. Patrick got away with yelling. I could yell, too. I wrenched his hands toward mine, trying to free my glider. The wings snapped off while the body crashed to the floor.

I didn't save my work.

Instead, I pulled the cord that started the engine inside my cousin.

"But it's not fair!" came even louder and from somewhere darker inside him. He was mad but not at me. Patrick jerked mightily from Uncle Mike's grip. He ran. Usually during these episodes, he somehow knew where the exit was and headed that way. Not tonight. He had a target at the other end of the room.

"It's not fair!" he screamed while running toward the launcher machine. All the ingredients for a Patrick moment were now in place. He had an audience, an unstoppable burst of energy, and something he could destroy. A few seconds ago, the Young Engineers probably thought creativity was his strong suit. They didn't know about his true gift. Destruction.

Mr. Grumbles's launching machine was a goner.

Within seconds, Patrick's outburst led him to the cart holding up the device. While not a big machine, I'm sure it wasn't light. None of the other kids knew how strong Patrick could be.

Or how scary.

It took minimal effort for him to heave the launcher to the gym floor. He created many pieces out of one.

Mr. Grumbles wasted no time in grabbing my cousin. He was no longer smiling.

"What is your problem?"

Patrick writhed like a fish on the dock, trying to escape his grip. Uncle Mike put a hand on Mr. Grumbles, allowing Patrick to escape and sprint to the exit door. The episode was almost over, but there were always aftershocks.

Mr. Grumbles shoved Uncle Mike.

"And what's *your* problem?" he shouted at my uncle for all to hear.

Uncle Mike had one foot in front of the other, shoulders slightly turned. It was his angry stance, the one that terrified me.

"What kind of father lets his kid act like that?" announced the leader of the Young Engineers, a group created to teach respect, sportsmanship, and honor. Even though he was mad, I think he still liked all the eyes on him.

"I'll show you what kin —"

"Mike!"

Dad. Dad saw that Mr. Grumbles was about to get

the scruff knocked off his face and stepped between the men, his hands on my uncle. "Patrick. We need to find him."

Uncle Mike broke his gaze from the leader of the Young Engineers and blinked hard.

"Right," he said to my dad. He looked at the faces watching, judging him. "We're done here." He marched straight to the same exit used by his son, and didn't return.

All eyes were on us now.

"We're leaving, too," Dad sternly told the room.

The walk back to our table took forever. A crowd's attention can so quickly make time stand still.

"All right, everyone, looks like we have two fewer members now!" Mr. Grumbles announced, his smile returning. Several of the dads laughed and began sharing perspectives of the scene that unfolded before them.

"Jimmy, get your things. Get Patrick's, too. Now," Dad said to me, but looked at Mr. Grumbles.

I gathered our supplies and stuffed them in my bag. Everyone was talking about us, parents and kids alike, as if we weren't in the room. I'm not sure I've ever felt less respected.

We left the gym, the onlookers, and the Young

Engineers as quickly as possible. Dad was breathing heavily when we got in the car.

"Should we help find Patrick?" I asked.

"No." His tone let me know to stay quiet until we got home. When we stopped in our driveway, he turned off the car, unbuckled the seat belt, and paused before looking at me.

"That's why you don't interfere."

Understood. Lesson learned.

When you stand up to Patrick, it only adds an earthquake to the tornado.

I hated when Patrick ruined things, but that night was different. He wasn't the one who cheated or got an award because his dad was in charge. But he was still the one ostracized from the group. I felt sorry for him.

Even though he was right, no one would listen to him.

Especially me.

*CHAPTER 5

Poor social skills can get amplified.

Will I pass out if these pants cut off enough of my circulation? If I pass out today, there's no way they could force me to do the speech.

All right, that's my plan. Hope for a small medical emergency and then I won't have to give the —

"Jimmy James," someone calls out. A wave of relief wipes across my face. I know the voice, and for the first time since the wake started, it's a voice I'm glad to hear.

"Chang Gang," I respond before even turning around. Every figure in the room goes dark as I see the light of a familiar face. "Hey! Wow . . . thanks for coming."

Victor Chang. He and I used to be pretty tight. In fourth grade, the two of us got into making our own comics. We even had a multi-issue series called *Cuddles, the Killer Gerbil.* They were always just inappropriate enough that we had to keep them hidden from Mrs. Horowitz. He had the art skills; I was the storyteller. We were a good team.

I hadn't hung out with him much since grade school, though. Partly because that's what happens in junior high, partly because of Patrick. Mostly because of Patrick. We were still friends, but what I call school friends.

"Yeah, the parental units said we should." His thumb hitchhikes toward his parents, talking to Dad. "So here we are," he says with one eyebrow up.

Victor is a good guy: a better artist than anyone in school but he'd never flaunt it. His parents are tough on him, and it makes me appreciate that mine aren't so bad. Even with perfect grades, he was always with some kind of tutor and usually had Chinese school on Saturdays. I think all that pushing is what made him have a bit of an edge. Maybe that's why we clicked.

"So this is . . . weird." Most people can't pull off calling something weird without sounding a little off themselves. Victor can.

"Yeah, been a weird day." I'm so glad he's here.

"So what do you do? Just stand around and talk to people?"

"Pretty much. A lot of small talk and 'I'm sorry's.' "

His cocked eyebrow returns to starting position.

"And you're here all day? Man, that sucks."

"Yup. Tell me about it. At least I get out of school for a couple of days."

"This actually got me out of my cello lesson, so I'm not complaining." His neck cranes to look past my shoulder. I know what he sees before he even asks.

"Is that him?"

"Yup."

"That's really him?"

"Yup. Want a closer look?"

"Um." Wrinkles form around his eyes as my question takes any lightheartedness out of his voice. "No. I'm good." His gaze continues past me to the open casket. "That's crazy. Wow. That's really him."

"I know. It's funny to watch people when they see him. Some go right up and kneel down in front of his face; others won't leave the entrance once they see the body."

"It's creepy, man. I mean, I don't mean that disrespectfully. It's just —"

"It's fine." I hold one hand up. "It is creepy."

"It's so crazy . . . what happened." Victor is scanning the room, looking for something to focus on besides the body.

"Yeah, I still can't believe it."

"Was it really an hour before they found him?"

"I guess so." Why is my heart beating faster? It's just Victor.

"Was he even on a team?"

"Not yet." And why am I breathing funny? "His parents thought he should learn to skate a bit, then maybe join a team."

He glances to the side. It's the same look he gets when he's not sure how to draw something.

"I thought, you know, team stuff wasn't a good fit for him." Victor doesn't miss much.

"It wasn't. But my uncle thought a sport that encourages checking your opponent into a wall might be a good place for him." Pretty sure I'm sweating now. And blinking more than I need to. "Guess we'll never know."

The details of Patrick's death are something almost

every guest has skirted around. As Victor is bringing it up, I realize that I'm no different and wonder if my anxiety thinks that, too. I think he picks up that it isn't the best topic.

"So after tomorrow morning, you're done, right? Just sit through the funeral?"

"Not exactly. I have to give a speech." Hearing the words only makes my stomach twist more.

"You have to give a . . . ?" His eyes scan for the word.

"A eulogy. Yup. That's exactly what I have to do."

"Sucks to be you. What are you supposed to say?"

"No idea. I'm supposed to tell a nice story about Patrick."

His eyes open slightly wider. "Well, good luck with that. Oh, hold on. My mom's flagging me. I'll be right back." With one hand waving slightly toward us, Mrs. Chang is signaling him to join her. She's nice enough but always intimidates me. I'm going to hang back and slow down my pulse and try to collect myself where the crowd isn't as dense.

Victor's feet never rest when he reaches his mom. He turns sharply back around to find me again.

"Hey, my mom wants you to come say hi."

Mrs. Chang was like that: very nice, very assertive.

"She does? Uh . . ." I really don't want to dive back into the sea of people.

"You're the reason we came, so, yeah, she wants to say hi."

"I am?" The thought of someone being here today for me never entered my mind. "Sure. Let's go."

Victor and I make our way through the masses again, which have already increased in a short time. A large group arrives, dividing the room, preventing me from seeing Mrs. Chang.

They walk through the entrance in a formation — has to be a dozen of them, all looking around the room. The way their eyes move through the guests, it doesn't look like they see who it is they're looking for.

Ranging in age, the group is a mix of fancy suits and casual sweatshirts. The last one, a particularly older man in tattered sweatpants and a maroon sweater, looks like one of those old guys who spend their days wandering public libraries.

The elderly woman leading them can't be ninety pounds soaking wet, but she moves fast and carries herself like a lumberjack. She looks at the growing line of guests for a second, then makes her way to the center of the room. The group follows, pauses, and continues scanning the faces.

They're not family — I would have recognized them. Friends of my aunt's? Can't be — Aunt Rose's friends are my mom's friends. Maybe Uncle Mike's coworkers? Whoever they are, they don't seem at all interested in waiting in the guest line.

Mom walks from the back entryway to greet them.

"Hello, I'm Lily Fitzgerald," she announces while approaching the front of the group.

No response. Not one of them moves. The scanning continues. Who are they looking for? Mom stops where she is, waiting for them to acknowledge her. Nothing.

Victor and I remain still and glance at each other as the caravan holds firm. His eyebrow is back up, a give-away that he's as interested as I am to see where this goes.

Mom circles to the front, cutting them off from moving forward. I wonder if she's worried they're at the wrong wake and doesn't want another Betsy incident. This time she's in front of the leader, her hand out-stretched to introduce herself. They can't ignore her now.

"Hello, I'm Lily Fitzgerald," she announces again, with a bit less friendliness.

140

The leader looks Mom in the eye while her index finger moves up, touching her own ear. She extends her other hand to meet Mom's. The handshake lasts only a second, as the woman pulls her hand back and above her head, waving feverishly at someone.

A tiny hand responds.

Standing alongside her parents is Sofia, her eyes big enough to reach her curly brown hair. The group's collective shoulders subtly drop a notch.

That's it. The group must be from Sofia's school. That's why they didn't respond to Mom the first time. They're deaf.

Mom turns to Sofia. Before she can ask a follow-up question, all of them shift their focus to my little cousin making her way toward twelve smiles that came for her.

The leader sidesteps Mom, and the group follows. Sofia hurriedly finds her way to the lumberjack in a navy-blue pantsuit, who is bending down just enough to gather my cousin in her arms. Each member of the group waits their turn for a hug from a beaming nine-year-old girl. Sofia now commands her own line in the center of the room.

Seeing how excited she is for each one of them is

really something. I would never look like that if a group of my teachers walked in. All these adults holding her up with their smiles — no wonder she loves going to school.

After everyone has their turn, the group breaks formation and huddles around Sofia with her wide eyes and unstoppable grin. The leader and Sofia connect with a flurry of words exchanged with hands and expressions, while the rest of the group absorbs Sofia into their mix until she can't be seen at all.

A few more words are exchanged, and one by one, the group peels away to reveal my cousin in the center. She points to my aunt and uncle by the casket. Guiding the leader, Sofia brings the group to her parents.

The family who was next in line waits in their place. I'm not sure anyone is going to object to Sofia bringing her friends to the front after what everyone saw.

Aunt Rose says hello first. The leader turns, giving my aunt her full attention while swiftly bringing a thumb to her chest, making a circle, then a series of other motions with both hands. I recognize "sorry" but don't get anything else. I suddenly feel a little ashamed for not spending more time learning ASL for Sofia.

Aunt Rose very promptly responds with her hand

coming down from her chin. *Thank you.* I know that one, too.

The leader signs to Aunt Rose again but is saying more. A lot more. Whatever she's saying is well beyond my level of ASL, but her expression says enough. She looks very concerned, very sorry for them. Her chin tucks slightly down while her hands rest to wait for my aunt's reply.

Aunt Rose does a side-eye for a second, then signs "Thank you" again.

The leader's head is tilted to one side, her eyes still fixed on my aunt. They don't look as empathetic now, more like teacher eyes. Each member of the group is locked in on my aunt. They're seeing something the rest of us don't yet.

Sofia, still next to her teacher, is biting her lip. Whatever it is, she sees it, too.

The leader takes a deep breath, readjusts her head, and the hands go to work again. A much shorter message is conveyed to my aunt and uncle, this time at a slower pace. She finishes signing and waits for a response.

My aunt and uncle stand frozen.

I look at the rest of the group, at Victor, and at the line of guests behind them. Without saying a word, the skinny elderly leader has commanded the attention of the entire room. All eyes are on my aunt and uncle, waiting for a response.

Aunt Rose turns to my uncle for a translation, but his open jaw and blank stare say enough.

She signs "Thank you" again, with quiet panic in her eyes. They match Sofia's.

The leader shifts back to Sofia and says something, at the faster pace, and ends with her index finger in a hook. I know that one, too. She just asked Sofia a question.

Sofia's hands don't budge. She keeps her sight connected with the leader's, but she is not answering whatever question the teacher just asked her.

The leader purses her lips. I think she got her answer.

My aunt and uncle's lack of effort to master ASL with their daughter is brought to light as the stranger in navy blue glares at them as if they were misbehaving children in her class. They know some basics, enough to tell Sofia it's time for church or to brush her teeth, but a detailed conversation is clearly not happening at the dinner table.

Despite being much shorter, the leader looks down on both my aunt and uncle; anger is finding its way into her expression. Her breathing starts to pick up as her hands come up again. Even though I wouldn't be able to understand her, I would not want to be on the receiving end of what she's about to say.

She starts in again, her hands not slowing down this time. No more than a few words are signed before she stops. Her hands freeze, as if something is keeping her arm from moving.

Something is.

Sofia has her hand on the leader's sleeve.

The anger in her eyes starts to dim as she looks down.

My cousin looks to the entire group of twelve and her hands start again. As Sofia is speaking to her friends, I try my hardest to understand what she is telling them. I only catch the last word, the one where each hand makes an L and comes together.

Brother.

The leader exhales a large breath.

The tight-knit group keeps their attention on the person they came for, each of them nodding once. Sofia moves between her friends and her brother, the way someone stands when they make an introduction. She leads them a few steps to the left, where Patrick's picture rests next to the casket. The leader turns toward the picture and bows her head. The rest follow, bowing their heads in unison, praying louder than anyone in the room.

Each of the twelve makes the sign of the cross at their own pace and waits for the others. They form a half circle, taking turns hugging Sofia to say good-bye. Her friends move toward the exit and follow their leader in navy blue out of the room.

The last of the twelve is the old man wearing tattered sweatpants and a maroon sweater. He pauses for a moment and turns back toward Sofia. Her hand comes up to her chest, fingers outstretched while waving in a more subtle way than before. Her hand says good-bye, but her smile and grateful eyes say so much more to her friend. The old man in the maroon sweater smiles back, waves, and follows his group out the door.

Sofia is like that. She has a way about her that brings out a person's gentle side, even when they're angry.

She could do that with her brother.

Usually.

A few summers ago, it was the hottest I can remember. Victor was at our house for the afternoon, and Mom was almost ready to agree to him sleeping over. My parents love Victor. He's that friend who whenever his name is mentioned, it's always followed by "What a nice boy" or "Such nice manners for a ten-year-old."

She kept suggesting we play outside, but we found the calm of air-conditioning and video games too enticing. That changed when she told us company was coming.

"Your aunt will be here in a few minutes. Are you sure you don't want a Popsicle outside?"

Oh, no. Just because you packaged bad news in a Popsicle doesn't mean I didn't hear it.

"Is she coming alone?" I knew the answer, but I hoped.

Mom was helping Aunt Rose choose paint colors for their bathroom. So that meant Victor and I had to entertain my cousins.

"Patrick and Sofia will be here, too." My face did not hide my feelings. Patrick loved coming over. I'm not sure if it was because of us, though. I think he liked any reason to not be in his own house.

"Tell you what, why don't you all take Victor to Gerald's for a treat. How does that sound, Victor?"

Smart move. Asking polite Victor if the plan is OK

with him, knowing he'll agree. Fine. A trip to Gerald's wasn't a bad compromise for the company we had to bring along.

"That sounds great. Thank you so much," Victor responded. He was abnormally polite with adults, and they loved him for it.

Ten dollars was the usual bribe for me to run to Gerald's Drugs for a treat with my cousins. Patrick liked it best when it was just the two of us, but he knew this was a package deal. Sofia usually came with us, and for the price of ten dollars, we got to pick out whatever we wanted.

Since Victor was joining the group, Mom upped it to twenty dollars. She expected us to take our time and didn't hold back reminding me of it. Sometimes we would go to the creek and look for bullfrogs; other times we would walk to the park on Edison Street to see if the metal slides were too hot to touch.

Once they arrived, Aunt Rose wasted no time scurrying us out. She wasn't good at hiding it when her limit was reached with Patrick. So the group made its way to Gerald's with the promise of sugar and freedom ahead.

Walking to Gerald's was routine to us. Patrick usually talked the whole trip while I pretended to listen as best I could. His rants usually began with an "If I only had a _____" statement and went in any direction from there. The blank was typically filled in with some fantasy item, like a pet shark or a Civil War cannon.

Even though Victor was polite, that didn't mean he was shy. He had no problem squelching Patrick's ideas. Patrick started talking about the possibility of silver in the ground, and if he mined the right places, he would be rich. Victor informed him of the costs, dangers, and low success rate of mining. Patrick could spout back just enough information to keep the debate alive. The two of them were full of random facts and had a mutual respect for each other's brains.

They carried on while I just listened. Sofia was content to take her place two strides behind us. She looked as if she were on a tiny carriage with us as horses pulling her toward a destination.

On a day like this we all knew the money would be spent on two things — ice cream and soda. We walked into the store and immediately made for the cooler. Gerald's was one of the last locally owned stores in town. The servers made small talk with whomever they wanted, scooped ice cream without wearing hairnets, and, best of all, sold soda in glass bottles.

Victor and I pulled out root beers, and Patrick grabbed his Dr Pepper. Sofia waited patiently at the ice-cream counter, peering into the frosted glass to scan the offerings. She knew there wasn't a decision — it would be mint chocolate chip like every time. Still, she liked to make the other flavors think they had a chance.

Patrick always chose his selection by looks and not taste. If the Superman flavor was available (which had nothing to do with Superman), he picked it because it had blue in it. If it wasn't, he went with strawberry. If you asked him what his favorite flavor was, he would tell you butter pecan without hesitation. I never saw him pick butter pecan. That was Patrick. You never knew what he was going to do.

We walked out of Gerald's, working on our ice cream with drinks in hand. Our frozen treats began to lose shape as soon as we crossed the threshold back into the sun. Some days we walked to our next destination while enjoying our dessert, but today we decided to sit on the curb so we didn't lose any of our ice cream to the pavement. We sat down, bearing the punishment of the heat, knowing that in three minutes our cones would be devoured anyway.

"Let's go to the creek. I bet I can skip one over it

today," Patrick said with excitement. The creek isn't big, but it feeds into a small retention pond. Once we learned how to skip rocks, it's given us many lazy afternoons of entertainment. Patrick was determined to skip one clear across the pond and was getting close to that goal.

"It's more about the rock you pick than how you throw it," Victor replied, welcoming a friendly discussion.

While Patrick was going on about his perfected throwing style, Sofia plopped next to me, very focused on her mint chocolate chip. She always stayed close to us in public. She wasn't fully aware of her surroundings and avoided interacting with people who didn't realize she was deaf. If she ever walked away from us, it was for an animal.

About three car lengths away, I saw a chocolate Lab leashed to the parking sign, waiting patiently for its owner to return. I knew Sofia couldn't resist.

My little cousin shares a bond with animals I've never seen in others. I like dogs, but with the exception of puppies, they scare me. Sofia could look a snarling Rottweiler in the eye with no fear and help the animal find inner peace. She's a magnet for all kinds of creatures, but dogs especially love her.

Patrick was now talking about pelicans and how

they'd be pretty easy to hunt, while I watched Sofia connect with the animal that easily outweighed her. It was an impressive exchange. The dog immediately recognized that a friend was approaching but didn't get overly excited. Its ears moved back, as if it were preparing for a race. As Sofia got closer, the dog's tail wagged harder in anticipation of meeting this kind face. She stood in front of the beast with her fingers extended for the dog to sniff. You could almost see imaginary hands shaking between them.

It was ninety degrees in the shade and even hotter on that sun-drenched curb. I knew that when Sofia met this animal, in its fur coat, she thought of nothing else but to share her ice cream to help it cool off. Most people would fear their hand would be taken by an eighty-pound dog when waving ice cream in its face, but Sofia knew her friend wouldn't do that. The dog looked at Sofia as if to ask permission. It calmly turned its head, and in one bite the ice cream disappeared off the cone. When she talks to animals, they listen. It's when Sofia shines brightest.

Behind me, simultaneous and aggressive voices shouted, "Hey!"

Patrick, Victor, and I turned to see two girls walking

toward Sofia. "That's our dog! She's not supposed to have ice cream!"

I recognized them from school. The Striker sisters.

They were a year ahead of me and lived a few blocks away. Not sure they would recognize me, but I certainly knew them. No one ever called them by their names (Megan and Mary, I think). They were just known as the Strikers. They were pretty, well liked by boys, and always together.

A memory of them walking behind Curtis Frey, the biggest kid in my class, while waddling with their arms and cheeks expanded, popped into my head.

"That's our dog! Who said you could give her ice cream?" The Strikers were on either side of Sofia now. She was still kneeling at the same level as her new friend.

"Who?" they demanded.

Sofia looked up at them, uncertainty in her face. The Strikers each took a step to complete their circle around Sofia and now stood between her and the dog. The connection was broken.

Sofia's hands fluttered. One hand still held the cone, while the other attempted to sign. There was no chance they could understand signing, and she could only mimic something that looked like an apology.

153

I set the bottle of root beer down to stand up and help. Immediately, Patrick gripped my forearm. He stopped talking. He didn't look at me, only at Sofia. She looked back at him, her eyes begging for help, with a newly formed tear.

He didn't move, just stared at his sister.

He was talking to her. He was telling her to not be afraid and to deal with this herself.

Victor looked at me, waiting to follow my lead as I followed Patrick's. I remembered overhearing my parents fighting once about our neighbors and the way Mr. Hendrix treated his wife. My mom just kept repeating, "You never get involved with someone else's family." Just like Grandma Mutz said: *Never interfere.* That rang in my head as I watched Patrick forcing Sofia to help herself out of this problem. I wouldn't interfere.

"Didn't you hear me? Answer me!"

Sofia didn't whimper, but the tear streamed down one side of her face. She was trying to be strong.

"Who said you could feed our dog ice cream?"

Sofia looked at the ground and then back at the accusers. I saw her chin rise first, then the rest of her. The Strikers were still two heads taller. She looked between them, at Patrick. The Strikers still hadn't put it together that we were with her.

Patrick let go of my arm, but his gaze was still locked on his sister. In the slightest of gestures, he nodded. Just once. Sofia took a breath, the kind that requires great effort. It was clear to me now that Patrick and Sofia had been in this situation before and had some kind of arrangement — one where Sofia wasn't getting an equal vote.

I knew what was coming and my stomach hurt. Patrick wanted Sofia to talk. He wanted her to use what language ability she had to stand up for herself. I could understand his intentions, but I also trusted my aching gut that this would end badly.

She picked a Striker to look in the eye. The one on the left. Sofia exhaled the breath and released it with the words "I'm sorry."

Since losing her hearing, Sofia speaks only when necessary and only around those she feels comfortable with (a total of five people). I don't fully understand how being deaf affects someone's speech. I just know what it's like when she tries to talk. It sounds like she has a full glass of lemonade in her mouth and the sugar and lemon are at war. The words want to get through without being garbled but just can't.

I've been around Sofia my whole life, before and since she went deaf. Even though she rarely uses her voice, when she does, I can understand what she's saying. I can do it with patience and understanding. The Strikers had neither.

I can't remember what the Strikers said in response to Sofia's apology, but both turned on her at the same time with a flurry of insults. At her left and right she was blasted with a variety of phrases mocking her speech. Deaf or not, Sofia heard the attack loud and clear.

Patrick got up, as quiet as his sister. He didn't run toward them. There was no need to hurry because what he had planned was going to happen no matter what. I stood up to follow, unsure of how Patrick was going to intervene but certain the results would be ugly.

The Strikers had been so caught up in the barrage of name-calling that they still hadn't pieced together that Patrick was connected to this girl with slurred words. Even as he approached them, they continued to blast Sofia, who'd given up on the life lesson her brother was trying to teach her.

Patrick moved like he was on rails that ended at the

twins. The Striker on the right was closest to the curb, closest to us. It was unlucky placement for her. She was the one to get hit.

It wasn't that I never noticed Patrick still had his bottle of Dr Pepper in his hand; it's that I never noticed he walked toward them carrying it like a Louisville Slugger. It was at his side the whole time, but the unopened narrow part was gripped in his palm, while the wide bottom hugged his shorts like an extension of his arm.

Without breaking stride, he took a mighty swing of his right arm and landed the bottle on the Striker girl's jaw. She didn't cry or fight back, just hit the pavement like — like she'd been hit in the face with a glass bottle. The other Striker sprinted away, leaving her sister and dog on their own. She hit flight mode and was gone.

My feet wouldn't move at first. I didn't know where to go. Sofia was sobbing, the dog was jumping in place, and the Striker was lying facedown on the sidewalk. I put one foot in front of the other and made it to the girl bleeding on the pavement. She rolled over, sobbing in pain.

Sofia tried to walk away, but Patrick grabbed her

forearm, the same way he had mine earlier. He stared at her until she stopped crying and then let go.

He wasn't finished with the Striker on the ground.

"You owe my sister an apology." He wasn't out of breath and didn't raise his voice, just spoke as though he were collecting on a bet between friends.

The girl held her hand to her cheek, wincing with pain. Her cries were muffled, scattered. I realized it was more than just the pain.

Patrick had broken her jaw. She cried hard and begged me with her eyes to stop this. I guess she recognized me after all.

"Apologize. Now," Patrick said again, still clutching the bottle.

I got it then. His goal wasn't to hurt her. It was to make her speak when she physically couldn't, just as she had done to Sofia. I had no idea if he was going to hit her again. I was certain that between the tears, pain, and shock, this girl wouldn't be able to form words.

Patrick's eyes never left the Striker girl's face.

"You owe my sister an apol —"

Patrick paused, turned to his side. Sofia took his weaponized hand in hers. Without words, she told him enough was enough and led him away from the mess of a girl he'd created.

He didn't get more than a few feet before one of the workers from Gerald's came out with the other Striker. He grabbed Patrick by the back of the neck and dragged him inside, yelling something about the police and his parents.

I checked on Sofia while she wiped a tear away. We walked back to our spot on the curb before I remembered Victor. He just got a front-row seat to my family and hadn't said a thing yet. He was still staring at where my cousin beat a girl in the face with a bottle. It took him a second to find words.

"What do we do?" he asked.

An hour earlier, I'd been in comfortable air-conditioning, playing with my friend and thinking he was going to sleep over. Now I was dripping with sweat between my crying cousin and a shell-shocked artist trying to figure out how to handle Patrick's assault charges. That's what happens when you add Patrick to a recipe. Things blow up.

"We're leaving. We need to get Sofia home." I didn't know if this was the best thing to do, but I had to be the one to make a decision. And I didn't want to be around if Patrick's behavior escalated even more.

By the time we got back to the house, Aunt Rose had already gone to pick up her son and deal with the aftermath. Being a paramedic, Uncle Mike knew a lot of the police in town and had been able to get Patrick out of trouble more than once. I had no idea if this would be one of those times.

Victor never came over again. We still talked at school, but nothing outside of it. It was kind of awkward between us. I didn't want to ever ask him about it. Partly because I didn't have any answers for my cousin, partly because I didn't want to hear my friend say he wouldn't hang out with me because of Patrick. I didn't blame him, though.

It was a few weeks before we saw Patrick again. Mom and Dad wouldn't tell me all that happened. I heard them talking about it a few times but only caught phrases like "uncontrollable behavior," and "his ups and downs aren't normal." Dad said something about Patrick needing help, the kind his parents couldn't give him.

Mom reminded him, with anger, that it wasn't our place to interfere.

*CHAPTER 6

Some people enjoy a wake like it's a wedding.

All the guests are dressed in uniform: black suits for the men, black dresses for the women. I doubt anyone has pants two sizes too small, like me, though. Standing in groups of three or four, the visitors have conversations that vary from tears to laughter. They somehow look both sad and festive. I still have no idea how to act.

Everyone seems to have a different emotion. Some ladies in the corner from Mom's cards club are laughing hysterically. Not politely chuckling, but shoulder-shaking laughter with their whole bodies. One of them is trying to get out what few words she can between laughs — sounds like a story about one of her kids making a mess. Maybe you're supposed to laugh at wakes and be happy for what you have.

Across the room, there's a lady looking over the pictures. She fixates briefly on each image, mumbling something to herself while nodding. I can't tell what she's saying, but she seems to remember every event. Her eyes are watery, her lower lip curled, and she's gripping a tissue in one hand. She reminds me of how Sofia looks when she scrapes her knee. I have no idea who she is.

"What a moron, right?"

This is new.

"I'm sorry?" I respond, getting my bearings on exactly who this is. And who is a moron?

"To do this . . . cause all this commotion," he continues.

Why don't people here say hi before starting a conversation?

"And for what?" he adds, blowing out a breath of annoyance. And whiskey.

Wait, I got it now — it's my dad's cousin, Phil. I don't know him well, but enough to know that my parents don't like him. I've only met him once before this. It was at a wedding a few years ago. He was drunk before the reception started. Mom and Dad don't see him often, but that's what happens when your license gets taken away three times. I'm completely lost. What is he asking me? Who is the mor —?

"Look at his mother. Awful. To put her through this . . . just shameful." He isn't even looking at me. Even though he's twelve inches from my face, I'm not one hundred percent sure he's talking to me.

"Yeah, poor Aunt Rose." What do I say? I debate walking away, but he starts getting louder.

"I mean . . . who does that? By himself? What did he think would happen?"

As if his volume isn't enough, heads turning toward us let me know he's getting louder.

"I mean . . . seriously? It's cold out, but it's freakin' March. Some kind of idiot, right?"

"Um . . ." I can't do this. I need an exit.

"Now everyone is here"— he pauses while scanning the room —"for him." His tone is switching from loud to angry. "For being a moron."

Is this guy for real? Is he seriously mad at the kid who died?

"I . . . I don't really know what happened." How do I get away from this man?

He wipes the corners of his mouth where spittle has formed.

"Where were you when it happened, anyway?"

"I . . . I wasn't . . . uh . . ."

What am I supposed to say? I don't know why I wasn't with him!

"Not fair to his family. Not one bit." The angry tone meets the loud volume. "Here they are! All sad for him."

Should I just walk away? What if I do and he gets louder?

"And was he seriously out there wearing s —"

"Hey, Phil!"

Dad.

Thank God he heard his drunk cousin.

"How are you? You get to see Helen yet? She's just over there and wants to say hi." Dad puts his hand on Phil's back to firmly guide him away from me. He must have taken notes when Marty took Betsy away. I don't know who Helen is, and I don't care. Cousin Phil and his whiskey-fueled words are someone else's problem now.

I can't keep guessing what people are thinking and how to respond to them.

I need space.

I head toward the back, where it's less crowded. I get a couple of breaths in, then it hits me — more color than I've seen all day. Only one person in our family would dress for a funeral as if it were a picnic.

The room is about to change.

A lavender hat bobs through the threshold of the parlor. I can't see the face, but I know immediately who that hat belongs to.

She pauses at the entrance with my uncle Roy, soaking in what's about to be her moment. We don't see Dad's sister often, but there's no mistaking when Aunt Millie arrives.

It's well known in the family that Aunt Millie loves wakes. She loves the crowds, the emotions, and, most of all, being the person who can always bring out the waterworks in anyone. I've heard Dad make fun of his sister for a lot of things, like being a hippie or out of touch with reality, but he takes true joy in ridiculing her passion for the deceased.

Aunt Millie looks forward to reading the obituaries, a ritual I witnessed myself during her last visit. She scans for a recognizable name, and if she doesn't spot one, she puckers her lips inward and tilts her head

165

slightly. It's the same look Mom would give me when I struck out in Little League — a "Better luck next time" glance. When she was visiting us, Millie usually didn't find a name she knew. But then came those bittersweet days when she did recognize a name, whether an old school friend or her hairdresser's mother's plumber, and she would scrunch up her eyes and let her lower lip protrude in a sad pout. That face didn't last long, though. She soon made the mental checklist of what she needed to rearrange in her schedule to ensure she could be at that wake.

The sun doesn't miss rising; Aunt Millie doesn't miss wakes. If there was a job she could create and do better than anyone, this was it: Professional Mourner.

She usually gets under my skin. Nothing ever bothers her and she lives stress free, regardless of whatever disaster is happening nearby. She has her own little bubble and never leaves that happy place. But for some reason, I'm oddly comforted to see her today.

One big room packed with people, and no bride or second-grader getting First Communion to steal the spotlight — this is where Aunt Millie hangs her hat. In a sea of awkward faces and hand-wringing, she's the one person who looks right at home.

I hold my ground in one of the four chairs in the room. Aunt Millie is about to go to work. Time for me to learn how to navigate a wake.

She quickly ditches Uncle Roy, knowing he'll only slow her down. She begins working the room, heading toward my chair, which gives me a prime vantage point to observe the master. She approaches someone I think is from Aunt Rose's gardening club.

1. The Entrance
Scan the room, chin up. Look through the crowd, without looking at anyone directly. Pause for a moment (maybe to see if anyone approaches you first). Don't appear too eager to talk to people: because it's a wake, after all.

2. The Smile
This is the tricky one. You're trained to smile when you greet people, but what about at a wake, where it's a room with a dead body in it? At the same time, you don't want to make people sadder or cry even harder. No smile at all means you're a jerk, which you just can't be at a wake. Aunt Millie has it down — smile with your mouth, frown with your eyes. An absolute pro.

3. The Approach

Choose your target, make direct eye contact, and step toward the person you're going to pull from the herd. Make them feel that you are here for them and them alone. Make that person feel special.

4. The Contact

Apparently, as a woman, you hug everyone. Hold it for three seconds and say something mid-hug. I watch her hug three different people and whisper what seems to be "Taken too soon" to each of them. Must be her call sign. For guys it's different. I still don't know which guys I'm supposed to shake hands with or which guys to hug.

5. The Banter

Conversations are each less than a minute, and she says almost the exact same thing each time:

— *What a tragedy.*

— *You look great.*

— *How is _____? (spouse/child/parent)*

— *We need to meet again soon under better circumstances.*

Each of these phrases is said with soulful eyes and constant nodding.

6. The Release

Hug. Again. But this time find a hand. Hold it with both of yours (one over, one under), making a sandwich of theirs, for about ten seconds. Tell them again how good it is to see them and how much their support means to the family.

This last part is by far the toughest part to maneuver. But Aunt Millie sees this challenge as an opportunity. While most people simply say good-bye, Aunt Millie lets you know that she sees you and that your time here didn't go unnoticed. She makes people feel at ease in a stormy sea of chaos. She enters a wake subtly yet takes over the room within minutes.

She's the Trojan horse of mourning.

Here she comes. Time to show her what I've learned.

"Hi, Aunt Millie." As I speak, I'm thinking about my lower face smiling while my upper face is frowning. I probably look like a Picasso.

"Oh, Jimmy." Her hug is tight, like it would support me if I fell but not hurt me. *One Mississippi, two Mississippi, three Mississippi* . . . "Been thinking about you, my dear. Your poor cousin was taken too soon. How're you holding up?"

"I'm OK. Been a tough few days." She now has my hand, sandwich-style.

"Look at this." Her left hand sweeps the room as if she held a wand, her right hand still holding mine. "If only your cousin could see this. Such a tragedy. So much life ahead of him."

Everyone's been saying things like this—"What could have been," "What promise in your cousin's life . . ." Either they didn't know Patrick or they're flat-out liars.

Aunt Millie goes through steps five and six with me before eyeing her next contact. But then comes the seventh step, which I didn't see coming. She places her hands on my shoulders and calmly asks me a question.

"Are you ready for your speech tomorrow?"

How does she know?

Nothing gets past her at a wake.

She's looking into my eyes, seeing right through me. She's not asking if I'm ready; she wants to know if I'm scared. My eyes apparently don't lie as her grip tightens and moves down my arms.

"No."

That's all I get out. One word. My speech is tomorrow, and I can't even manage a complete sentence.

"You'll do great," she assures me while rubbing my arms. "Just speak from the heart, dear." Her words are reassuring, but her eyes scream, "Better you than me."

She gives me one last pat on the shoulder before walking away and reaching out to the next guest in her path. This isn't a wake to Aunt Millie. It's a buffet. She picks up her plate at the door and goes down the line sampling something from each person in front of her.

Speak from the heart. Great advice from someone not giving a speech tomorrow.

I need space.

I go back into the hall and find it empty, except for Sofia, whose back is to me. She's looking over the empty tray of cookies, hoping to find one she's missed. Her hand lifts the tray to see if there's a secret cookie waiting underneath. In her other hand is a swinging Norman, her safety net.

I could use a safety net. And some pants that don't cut off my circulation.

I can't blame her one bit if that walrus doesn't leave her grip until tomorrow is over. She's lucky, though. Most people aren't trying to talk to her. She also doesn't have to give a speech tomorrow.

Am I an awful person for thinking that? What is wrong with me? Here is my nine-year-old cousin, who has probably never had any experience with death, and I'm complaining.

This is her first wake, too. She must be so overwhelmed.

While this is my first wake, at least it's not my introduction to death.

I have Aunt Millie and Uncle Roy to thank for that.

I learned early in life that the word *vacation* can mean different things to different families. Some families go to Hawaii or on a ski trip. Our family vacations were always to see relatives, not destinations. As an eleven-year-old, a trip was a trip to me, and I always looked forward to them no matter where we went.

I didn't know a lot about my aunt Millie and uncle Roy. They never had kids, for some reason, and I wasn't allowed to ask about that. I also wasn't allowed to ask why we hardly ever saw them. I'd overheard Mom and Dad talking about it once. Dad said something about her "hippie-dippy life" along with a few other colorful words regarding his sister. Mom told him it was time to put differences aside and that we were going to "make an effort," whatever that meant. Easter was next Sunday, so they figured it'd be a good time to go.

Roy and Millie live on a farm three hours away in a small town called New Basel. It's mostly farmland with a small downtown. "Downtown," like "vacation," is a relative term. The busiest corner of New Basel consists of a welding shop, a post office three people could fill, and the local bar, Floyd's. Traffic has never been heavy enough to warrant even a stop sign.

Only when we were an hour away from their farm did Mom tell me that her sister was coming. Which meant Patrick was coming.

Aunt Millie apparently tells everybody she sees, "You should come to the farm — you'd love it!" I always figured she was just saying it or being polite. Turns out that when Aunt Rose found out about our visit, she called Aunt Millie's bluff and e-mailed her, asking if they could come, too.

It's always been tough for us to ever do anything without Aunt Rose inviting herself. She has mild panic attacks whenever we leave town, so our excursions frequently turn into joint-family events. Maybe it's part of being a twin, but she isn't happy when Mom isn't reachable in person. Mom likes to play it off as a joke and say, "When you marry a twin, you marry us both!" I've never seen Dad laugh at this.

We pulled up to the farm just before bedtime and saw that my aunt and uncle had already arrived. I don't think Dad was in any hurry and planned it so we would get there late and go to bed. The four adults were sitting around the table with empty plates before them and a half-eaten strawberry pie in the center. My aunts were each having coffee, and my uncles beer. Uncle Mike usually didn't go to sleep until he had a few cans of what he called his "bedtime medicine" under his belt.

"Hello! Hello! Look who's here!" Aunt Millie said in a voice as if she were reading a book to a two-year-old. We exchanged hugs and handshakes before my parents took a seat at the table. "Pat and Sof are in the barn playing with the kittens," Uncle Roy said while pointing to one of the structures outside. I took the hint and went to find them while thinking about how much Uncle Mike hates it when people don't call his kids by their full names.

I'd never been to a farm before and never realized how many buildings there could be. I always thought there was a house you live in and a barn for the animals and that's it. Their farm had these, along with several giant sheds. The barn was dark, and I could hear animal noises. I didn't know livestock well enough to know which animals made those sounds. I stopped for a second to hear where they were coming from.

"Watch this! I'll make it a king on a throne!"

Patrick. He'd found the kittens. His voice came from one of the smaller buildings with a light on. Sofia had to be there, too.

I walked toward the entrance door, which looked big enough to drive a truck through. The building was one giant dirt-floor room with a path through the middle where tire treads marked the ground. An old U.S. mail jeep with four flat tires sat dormant in one corner. The jeep side also housed an assortment of metal objects, ranging from chicken wire to a small bulldozer. Standing on the front loader of the small dozer was Patrick, strategically placing kittens on top. Three were up there so far.

"This place is awesome!" Patrick exclaimed. "I checked for keys, but there's none in it. It's our safari truck. We're in Africa." Sometimes I knew Patrick's mouth couldn't keep up with his mind. "Look at the lions we found on safari!"

Poor kitties. I didn't think Patrick would hurt them, but I also knew he'd see how far he could go before they did get hurt. Sofia was sitting on an overturned bucket with her feet elevated. Two orange kittens were playing with her shoelaces. She smiled and waved to me. She was a better fit for kittens than her brother.

From behind me, someone screamed like they were in severe pain. It filled the room from what I thought were speakers in every corner. I instinctively jumped back, unsure of what made the hideous noise. I'd never heard a live farm animal before. It was kind of terrifying.

"They're back!" Patrick charged while removing the newly crowned kings off the dozer. "The rhinos are back!" He set the kittens down and marched toward the other side of the barn. I knew it wasn't going to be a rhinoceros, but the animal yelled loud enough to intimidate me. I looked at the pen to see a sheep making its presence known.

"Where did it come from?" I would've noticed this animal when I walked in. It was massive. I don't know what I expected when seeing a sheep this close for the first time, but not something I could easily ride. Then I heard the noise again, but it came from somewhere else. In the corner of the pen was an opening to the outside. Another sheep came sauntering into the building and butted up against the one close to us. It was slightly bigger than the first and strutted as though it were the boss of the two. It opened its mouth and screamed again. It wasn't cute like in cartoons. This animal made me rethink stepping any closer. Patrick leaned over to scratch its imaginary rhino-horn while I wondered if the sheep would bite.

"This one's Ginger," Patrick explained while moving his hand closer to the sheep's nose. "Aunt Millie said she's a show lamb and is going to win big at the fair this summer." Aunt Millie must have given a tour before we arrived. "And that's Slipper," he said, pointing to the smaller one. While she couldn't hear the aggressive sounds coming from the beasts like I could, Sofia kept a safe distance from the fence. "Check out her eye! It's so gross!"

I really didn't want to see it but was too curious. I took two steps and saw its one eye was completely sealed shut with pink skin in place of an eyelid. This lamb was taller and the more slender of the two, better resembling the gentle creature I pictured a lamb to be. I couldn't help but feel sorry for it.

177

"Aunt Millie said it got bit in the face as a baby. Said it's fine now, just has one eye." Patrick was now holding imaginary treats for Slipper to see if she would jump like a dog. She didn't. Ginger continued to let out horrible, torturous sounds. I shuddered every time Ginger shrieked. Sofia moved closer to me, curiously looking at Slipper.

"So . . . Slippers had —"

"Slipper, not Slippers," Patrick corrected me as if I'd called the sheep a horse. "And she's a rhino on our safari."

"So Slipper had an accident, but her eye doesn't hurt?" I extended my hand to let her smell me the same way I did with unfamiliar dogs. Sofia followed my lead and did the same. While I'm sure my face looked sour and hesitant, Sofia stared directly at the lamb and her damaged eye. Even though the other animals were bustling around, she and Slipper were locked in a calm gaze with each other.

"Nope. Aunt Millie said she's fine." Patrick was now trying to mimic Ginger's calls, and that only prompted her to scream even more.

Sofia had her hand open, completely vulnerable, in front of Slipper's mouth. The slender lamb sniffed for a moment and licked her palm. Sofia giggled. The moment was short-lived, as Ginger jealously shoved Slipper aside. Sofia's hand retracted just as quickly and her expression changed. Slipper turned away and lay down in the corner just as Aunt Rose's voice carried into the shed telling us to come in. She must have heard Patrick provoking the sheep and decided to end it. Sofia waved good-bye to her woolly new friend before we went inside to get ready for bed.

The next morning was Easter Sunday. This Easter was especially great because we were at the farm — the farm that was three hours from our church and the incredibly long Easter Sunday mass. Not going to Easter mass was better than anything the Easter Bunny might bring. Millie and Roy aren't religious and don't belong to any church. I knew it bothered Uncle Mike and Aunt Rose that we skipped church, but they kept quiet about it. Patrick was thrilled and shouted, "Happy Easter! No church! Thank you, Jesus!" at breakfast.

During the egg casserole, Aunt Millie said she'd set up an Easter egg hunt for us. We weren't allowed to look in the yard until she said so, and the one with the most eggs got a prize. I perked up at the mention of "prize." I'd never been in a real egg hunt and couldn't wait. I was amazing at finding Mom's keys and I felt good about my chances. We cleaned our plates and ran to the door to wait for the hunt.

Uncle Roy took Dad and Uncle Mike to show them something in one of the buildings. Mom and my aunts stayed to watch the hunt and gave each of us a basket. We stepped onto the porch, ready to go.

Eggs peppered the yard in every direction. Not really hidden, just scattered all over the lawn. They weren't colorful either. Aunt Millie explained that this was a farm-egg hunt, and these were real eggs so we needed to be careful with them. I knew Patrick wouldn't hesitate to hurt me to win, so I began strategizing. Maybe start far out then work back to the house? Before I could come up with a plan, Aunt Millie shouted out, "GO!" and we were off.

I darted to the farthest egg I saw. Past the gravel driveway and to the fence. Got it. Now to work my way back. I crouched low, scouring the grass for more. On my left, I saw Patrick do exactly as I predicted and go for what was in front of him. He was shouting, "Another ostrich egg! Africa is full of ostrich eggs!" as he picked them up. Sofia was being led by Aunt Millie to some of the less obviously placed eggs. Six were in my basket now. If I moved quickly, I could double that before Patrick got the rest.

What sounded like one of Woody's illegal fireworks abruptly sliced through the egg hunt. Not a series of pops, more of a cannon being fired, once, in the distance.

I dropped my basket and jumped up to a standing position. Patrick was to my left, also standing tall, with one hand clutching his basket and the other stopping an imaginary punch. Sofia hadn't broken stride and was reaching for another egg. I looked at my basket, which was now leaking yolk from the fall.

What was that? A firecracker? Mom and Aunt Rose each had their hand clutching at something — Mom grabbed the porch rail and Aunt Rose grabbed Mom's arm. Sofia and Aunt Millie were completely unfazed.

Dad and Uncle Mike came from behind one of the sheds. No Uncle Roy.

"What was that?" Patrick yelled in excitement. He liked things that went boom.

Dad and Uncle Mike didn't look excited. Dad looked like he did when he saw the spoiled food in the garage freezer when it shorted out. Uncle Mike looked less unnerved, but not by much.

"What was that?" Patrick asked again. Sofia and Aunt Millie continued to work toward their sure win at the egg hunt, while I stood waiting for answers.

"Nothin'. Just keep finding eggs," Uncle Mike said gruffly while he approached our moms. "Just stay put." Dad was staring at Mom while walking hurriedly toward her, his eyes wide enough to put me on edge.

When Dad reached the porch, he talked with his hands the way he did when he was charged up about something. Whatever he said, Mom put her hand over her heart.

Animals, prizes, and a small explosion . . . this was too much for Patrick — even I knew that.

Aunt Millie was making her way to the porch with Sofia. She still wasn't alarmed by either the noise or that everyone else was visibly upset.

I walked my dripping basket toward them and heard Dad saying, "A little warning would have been nice," to Aunt Millie. Her head cocked to one side the way her collie's does when he hears the screen door open. Her eyes didn't look curious, though, more offended, like Dad had just asked her how much she weighs.

"We thought it would be a nice treat for everyone. You can't do something like this where you live. Just wait until you taste it. Roy can perform miracles with a smoker, and once you —"

"I'm sure it's great, Millie, but Christ, we didn't need to see it get shot in the face before Roy slit its throat," Uncle Mike said, cutting her off and forgetting I was behind him.

And Patrick behind me.

"We thought lamb would be a nice treat for Easter Sunday dinner. I know it's not the same as picking something up at the store, but wh —?"

Patrick bolted at "lamb."

We all turned as he darted behind the building where the shot came from. Uncle Mike followed as best he could. We all knew he couldn't catch Patrick. That switch inside my cousin had been flipped.

Aunt Rose let out a sigh that indicated what all of us were thinking. Sofia's face channeled our concern as she watched her father sprint after her brother.

A few seconds later, Uncle Mike came from behind the building with my cousin in his arms. His limbs were flailing and he struggled to break his father's grip while he screamed, "It's not fair! Slipper was part of the safari!"

Uncle Mike had almost made it to the porch before

Patrick found a way to squirm out of his hands. Red-faced and breathing heavily, Patrick plowed through us and raced upstairs, where we heard a door slam.

Aunt Rose stood in the doorway before any of us could follow Patrick into the house. "I'll deal with it." She looked at her husband, who blew out a harsh breath and nodded. The seesaw was on its way down. They'd been here before.

We all waited on the porch, but we could hear everything. My cousin's words echoing through the farm could not be contained. Layered between Aunt Rose's "Come out from there" and "It's all right" came Patrick's fury-laced shouting we'd all heard before.

"Why did they kill it?"

Something was thrown against the wall. A book?

"Why did they name it and then kill it?"

Something was knocked over.

"Why did they name something they were going to kill?"

Something was punched.

"The other sheep are going to die!"

A lightbulb burst. He'd knocked over the lamp.

"Why do they eat animals they take care of?"

Something different hit the wall.

"How many animals have been killed?"

Stomping feet.

"Why are all the animals going to die?"

Quiet. He must be under the bed again.

This went on for another twenty minutes until Uncle Mike went inside. He didn't go in to help, but to pack their things and load up the car. Mom and Dad stayed outside. Dad took a step toward the door, but Mom held his arm. He didn't say a word; he knew. She didn't want him to interfere. I pictured an imaginary Grandma Mutz standing over her, reminding her of the family rule.

Uncle Roy came back to the house a few minutes later and did his best to explain how good the fresh lamb would be, insisting that if they left, they'd be missing out.

That's the way Roy and Millie operated. They lived in their own happy place and chose to not acknowledge anything bad around them. Whether it was a slaughtered lamb or a screaming eleven-year-old boy who wouldn't come out from under a bed, they just forged ahead. I was piecing together why we didn't see them very much.

Aunt Rose eventually came downstairs with heavy

eyes. Patrick was out from under the bed but still not leaving the room. I knew my aunt and uncle just wanted to leave, but they were worried about Patrick having another episode. About an hour later, he did come downstairs, led by his mom. They didn't say good-bye or even stop walking until he was in the car. Uncle Mike already had the engine running and Sofia buckled in the back.

My parents followed their lead and insisted we leave as well. There was no point in pretending to enjoy Easter now. I could tell everyone wanted to go back home. Roy had already called some friends over "so the lamb wouldn't go to waste," and Mom and Dad said we needed to beat the traffic. We thanked them for letting us stay the night and climbed into the car. We were about to leave when Aunt Millie stopped us.

"I almost forgot! You won! You're the last one here, Jimmy, so looks like you get the egg hunt prize. Hold on . . ." she said while running back into the house. Dad gripped the steering wheel until his knuckles turned over the top. She came back with a paper bag.

"Here you go, Jimmy. I know you don't need it now, but it might come in handy next year. Made it myself."

"Thanks, Aunt Millie," I said as politely as possible.

I didn't know what to think of two people who would introduce a sweet animal to a group of kids, then expect them to eat it the next day. I wanted nothing to do with whatever was in the bag.

"You're welcome. Come back soon!" Aunt Millie said as she and Uncle Roy waved good-bye. As soon as we turned out of the driveway, Mom's curiosity got the best of her.

"OK, what is it? Open it," she said reluctantly.

I peered in the bag to see what my hippie-dippy aunt who loves wakes and slaughtering animals made for the winner of the egg hunt. It was a fitting prize to end a memorable Easter weekend.

The weather was too warm for it now, but maybe next year a wool scarf would come in handy.

*CHAPTER 7

You'll be surprised at who shows up.

Aunt Rose and Uncle Mike have been standing and smiling for three hours. It's so strange how many people smile at funerals. I don't know what I expected. Smiling for so many hours seems like it takes it out of you more than standing, though.

Everyone who walks through the door is here to see my aunt and uncle. I feel bad for them. That's a lot of polite conversations about their son's death. Aunt Rose is swaying a bit, not standing firm like before. Mix in the crying with standing/smiling, and she may collapse soon.

The greeting line is still wrapped around the room. Most people who have gone through it are just hanging around in the middle now. It reminds me of a wedding we went to last summer. A huge line of friends and relatives, a quick hello and thanks for coming, then just hanging around, having awkward conversations with people you kind of knew and kind of wanted to see.

I notice something different in the far corner of the room. Something I haven't seen for hours.

Open space. A narrow gap between the end of the reception line and an older couple I don't know. It has to be a five-foot circle of daylight uncluttered by people and their voices. If I move now, I can make it. I just need a few minutes to try to think of a story to tell tomorrow.

Who was the god of moving unseen? Leto? Lelantos? Doesn't matter. That's what I have to do. The entire building is too full of people for me to find an empty room, so I need to be motionless among the crowd until they don't see me. That's it. Just make it to that small space of freedom, remain still, and avoid eye contact. Like a hunter in the wild, I'll become one with my surroundings.

I stealthily inch toward my prize until my feet are centered in the middle of the open space.

Did it work? At least thirty seconds have gone by, and no one has noticed me. I did it. My strategy is working. I'm hiding in plain sight.

I have some time. It won't last, so I have to take advantage. The crumpled paper with my partially written speech finds its way out of my pocket. The movement and noise of the crowd is still in range, but this will have to do. I have to write something down.

OK, Patrick.

Patrick, when I think of you . . .

Draft 2 of Speech

I didn't know if there was something wrong with him. I tried to spend time with him. It wasn't always easy. The truth is . . .

Two men walk in my direction.

No, not now. I need more time. I crumple my speech and stuff it into my sport-coat pocket.

Maybe they won't notice me. Remain still. Look through them. Be the wallpaper. They stop short of me, continuing their conversation.

It's working.

"See, that's the key to it all. A little more in the fall

goes far enough in the spring to keep it green," the older of the two is saying with his hands in front of his chest.

I know him. It's our neighbor Chucky from down the street. He loves talking lawns. He could go on for hours about which spring months are best for grass phosphates or how clipping disposal is the true sign of a green thumb. He and the other man stop close to me but haven't noticed my presence. I remain still, knowing any movement could trigger another awkward exchange.

"And some of these people, it's like they don't care if their lawn makes the rest of the street look bad! I remember when we had a —"

I don't consider myself claustrophobic when the walls are closing in, but people closing in, I can't handle that. These two are now blocking my only exit. I don't see a way out of this space if I need to move. I'm trapped.

"— committee that would make sure everyone kept their lawns proper. Not anymore," he says, shaking his head and looking scornfully at the floor as if that's the most tragic realization while standing twenty feet from the body of a thirteen-year-old boy.

It's getting harder to breathe. These pants aren't helping. What I wouldn't give for a pair of sweats right now.

"I hear ya," responds the other man. I recognize him, too. He's one of the insurance adjusters at Dad's office. I've known Tom Carlson for all thirteen years of my life, but I've only ever seen him at the agency's annual Christmas party. He's always jovial and typically full of beer and toffee. "Would certainly help property values."

Breathing is tough again. I need to move. No choice. Either of these men could grab me for another "How are you holding up?" talk, which I can't do right now.

I need to think.

I need to unbutton my pants.

I need space.

The men keep talking while my feet begin to carry me past them. Slow, steady, like a trained killer. Sip of breath, not too much, then slowly turn. Right foot, left, right again, no sudden movements. That's it. The two men are still engaged and I'm undetected. A few more steps and I'll be able to break for the bathroom. Three paces away, two —

"So . . ." A hand grabs me from the side.

Why is everyone working against me to write this speech? Wait. This hand feels smaller than the others.

"He ever find a picture for that frame?"

"What?" I'm lost. I want to physically hurt the next

person who starts a conversation with a question that throws me off.

"The frame he made. From carpentry club. Remember?"

Micah Carendini from school. Another person on the growing list of guests who skip formal introductions or hellos. Also, the only person who ever called Patrick a friend.

Micah moved here at two years old from Georgia (the one in Europe, not the South). He loved telling people he was from Georgia, only to correct them when they assumed it was the U.S. state. It was never a good first impression.

Micah is kind of a gangly kid, one whose bones have far outgrown the rest of his being. He has a demeanor where he looks at you a little too long and asks questions that are a little too personal. It makes people pretty uncomfortable, and it's likely why he is avoided by most other kids. I always saw a unique bond between my cousin and him.

"Carpentry club? Yes. Yes, I remember now. Um, no. I don't think that frame ever made it home," I say politely while wondering if he really forgot why Patrick and I stopped coming to carpentry club.

"Mine did. So did the birdfeeder I made when we got to pick our project. My mom keeps it inside, though. So the rain doesn't ruin it." His chest puffs slightly with confidence.

Micah has a quality about him that sets him apart from other socially awkward kids. His perception of himself and the reality of himself are completely disjointed. He loves to draw, specifically birds, yet has refused any kind of training or advice. He feels his natural gift is so refined that any feedback is scoffed at and usually followed by a personal assault. This went over horribly in art class last year. Miss Bickenstein told him he needed to follow the proper shading techniques they were using in class. He replied by reminding her of the lonely, unmarried life she was living.

He and Patrick did kind of click.

"Yeah, I wish we could have made it to the bird-feeder part." I don't know what else to say to him. I want to walk away.

"Once we were allowed to use the miter saw, it was a lot more fun. Some people were afraid of it. I don't know why. You just hang on to the board and it won't fly up. It's easy."

"Yeah, I'd forgotten about that," I say, trying to look

as if I weren't lying. "I guess we left the club too early."

The after-school carpentry club Patrick and I joined — and abruptly quit — last spring is not a memory I want to revisit now.

"I have Mr. Biner again this year. I told him about Patrick. He said he was sorry and that Patrick was a funny guy."

One of the first things I've learned about wakes is everyone speaks highly of the deceased. I'm amazed by how many people have commented on what a great kid Patrick was. He wasn't. His teachers especially hated him. To hear Mr. Biner say, "He was a funny guy," was his teacher way of saying he was a jerk. I doubt Mr. Biner thought he was a funny guy when Patrick assaulted him.

"Yeah, that's nice of him."

"I'll probably be president of carpentry club this year. You should try it again."

I don't have the energy to tell Micah that no such position exists. It wouldn't matter if I did. He would proclaim himself president at the first meeting and no one would bother arguing.

"I'll need a good vice president — not sure who is ready, though."

I don't know if there's a Greek god of misguided self-perception, but Micah would certainly have a temple for him.

"That's great."

I got nothing else. I need space.

"The seventh-graders won't know enough about what we do. They can't even use the machines at first. I need someone with experience." His face creeps slightly more toward me, into my precious breathing space.

"Yeah, good luck with that. Listen, I think my mom wants me to —"

"That's why I'm glad I ran into you today."

What? Ran into me? I don't care where this is going. I'm walking away before he asks me something really awkwa —

"I'd like you to be my vice president of carpentry club."

My face warms as blood finds its way up my neck. Everything that's happened since I stepped out of the car in my tight pants suddenly finds its way into my brain.

All. At. Once.

1. Be in a room with a dead body.

2. Give a speech tomorrow.

3. Make up nice things about your cousin.

4. Pretend you aren't scared of public speaking.

5. Talk to everyone when you don't want to.

6. Get cornered by everyone.

7. *Accept a made-up second-in-command position and take orders from Micah Carendini?*

That's it. Enough. No more.

"Are you serious? You're seriously asking me at my cousin's wake to be the vice president of a worthless after-school club?"

Micah's mouth is open, but nothing comes out.

"I'm sorry, Mr. President, but I'm a little busy right now! Is that what you came here for? Your stupid club?"

I wasn't aware my voice raised, but when the feet around me begin shuffling, I realize I've made a scene.

Micah stares at me.

"I . . . no." He takes a step back. "I came for Patrick."

Oh, no.

What did I just do? Those words just came out of me. My face is going from angry to embarrassed red.

"I . . ." is all that musters out. I just hauled off on Patrick's only friend, for no reason. Micah's eyes seem much clearer than a few seconds ago. They are seeing the shame forming inside me. I can't do this.

"I need to go."

I hurry past him, away from what was briefly a safe space, and back into the crowd. Being still didn't work; now I will just keep moving. At least until Micah leaves.

Vice president of carpentry club? Seriously? Why did that stupid request hit me so hard?

I'm walking from my own guilt. Micah wasn't trying to push me. It's just how he is. It wasn't his fault. I just . . . I can't be asked to do any more for anyone right now.

Still, I feel awful.

He came for Patrick. I know that. He was trying to be nice, in his own weird way. I didn't think that little request would have set me off like that, but I just lost it.

I snapped on someone who never saw it coming.

Maybe I have more in common with Patrick than I realized.

We spent the first week of carpentry club deciding on something to make. We had to plan it, get it approved, and set up materials. For a group of seventh-graders, it was a horrible tease to not let us touch any power tools until week two. When that meeting happened, we wanted nothing more than to hear steel blades cutting solid wood.

There were only six of us in the club, and we were waiting for Mr. Biner to arrive. We knew if we touched any of the tools before he entered the room, we were immediately kicked out. Mr. Biner walked in a few minutes late, looking a little flustered.

"Change of plan, boys. Gotta see a man about a horse. No carpentry club today," Mr. Biner said while jingling a large ring of keys. "It's storming bad out there, so if you don't have a phone, use the one in my office to get your ride here pronto." He was locking the drill cabinet with one hand while pointing to the phone with his other.

"Can we just build on our own?" Micah asked, seeing absolutely nothing wrong with a group of twelve-year-olds by themselves with a pile of circular saws.

"Nope, phone. Now," Mr. Biner replied, still pointing at his office.

"We know how to use the saws. We'll be fine." Micah picked up on social hints as well as Patrick did.

"That's twice I told you no. Not going to be a third. Get to those calls."

None of us felt like testing this man's temper, so we

all moved toward the office phone without argument. At least, five of us did.

"Why is it canceled?"

Patrick hadn't even turned his head toward the office. He had that look I'd seen many times. I dreaded it and knew what was coming.

Mr. Biner was twisting the lid on his coffee thermos and hadn't looked up. "Told ya, man about a horse." I couldn't tell if he was trying to avoid the conflict or truly didn't care.

"What does that mean?" Patrick shifted his ear toward Mr. Biner.

"It means my wife told me water is leaking into my basement, so I need to get home and see to it." He put the thermos in a bag. "So get on the horn and call, because I can't leave until all of you've been picked up."

Vivek Patel had just hung up and passed the phone to Peter Samington. I was third in line. Patrick hadn't even stood up. He turned back around on the stool, put his elbows on the table, and looked at the rain.

Within three minutes, all five of us had called home and Mr. Biner had his bag in hand. "Everyone got rides coming?" We all nodded and walked toward the door. "Patrick, you even call yet?"

Patrick's gaze didn't leave the storm. He responded with a shrug of his shoulders.

"Hey! I'm not playing games here! Get in the office and call now!"

The five of us stood back waiting for Patrick's next move. This was always so much worse with an audience.

Patrick responded quietly, talking to the window.

"I don't have a ride."

Mr. Biner dropped his bag and walked over to Patrick, who hadn't moved from his stool. Whenever Patrick got into it with someone, he did it head-on and never hesitated. Not this time. Something was different.

"What's your problem?" Mr. Biner's voice reminded me of the general in a war movie I'd seen Dad watch. "You think I'm playing games? Get up and make the call!"

Patrick didn't move.

"I wasn't supposed to be home until five o'clock. I don't have a ride."

"Then get up and find one!" Mr. Biner was now clapping his hands in Patrick's face as if he'd fallen unconscious. Patrick stood up but didn't look at his opponent.

"I'll just wait in the hall. I don't have a ride until five." He grabbed his backpack and turned toward the door.

201

I had to do something.

"I can give him a ride." Even though it was out of the way, I knew Mom wouldn't mind. "Patrick, my mom can take you."

"There . . . finally, an Einstein idea. Just hitch a ride with Jimmy. Let's go. Wait up front for your parents." As Mr. Biner made for the light switch, Patrick chimed in.

"Why can't I just wait here?"

Mr. Biner's eyes grew; his head tilted toward his shoulder. He stared at Patrick for a second.

"What is your problem? You dumb or something? There's no one else in the building. No one will be here, and I can't leave until you do. You're going home with Jimmy and that's that." He reached for the light switch. Rain is so much louder when you're hearing it in a silent, emotionally charged room.

"I'll just wait in the hall until five. I wasn't supposed to be home until then."

Mr. Biner didn't spend any energy to process Patrick's words this time. He didn't look confused or even like he were looking for a response. His hand grabbed Patrick's arm and shoved him through the doorway and into the hall.

My cousin didn't like to be touched.

Patrick instinctively yanked his arm upward to break Mr. Biner's grip. He was finally looking at his teacher for the first time since this began. The carpentry teacher smiled coyly and, with a shake of his head, muttered, "You really are dumb."

Mr. Biner had thirty years and eighty pounds on him. That didn't stop Patrick from using his palms like battering rams to shove his teacher up against the lockers.

Patrick's dominance lasted only a second as Mr. Biner righted himself — and Patrick along with him. In one swift motion, Patrick was spun around with his face shoved against the locker. His cheek began to merge with the three vents that stuck out as Mr. Biner pressed on the back of his head. He held my cousin hostage long enough for the five of us to see what it took to make a human being shrink.

He yanked Patrick's face away from the locker vents and pointed him toward the exit. Patrick ground his teeth and scowled through the three red marks on the side of his face. The rest of us exchanged looks of self-preservation, terrified we would be next. We obediently followed them to the exit, where Mr. Biner paused momentarily to mutter, "You're toast," with his hand squeezing the back of Patrick's neck.

In case Patrick didn't understand who'd won this fight, Mr. Biner gave one last reminder of his authority by using Patrick's body to open the door. The five of us helplessly followed until Mr. Biner slammed the door behind me and walked back inside.

There was just enough room under the overhang for us to stay dry while we waited for our parents. Everyone was picked up except for my cousin and me. Patrick wouldn't look at anything but the ground, his jaw still grinding. His eyes held tears, refusing to release them. I didn't know what to say, or who was really at fault here. Thankfully Mom's car turned the corner and this moment would be over soon.

"I see Mom. Let's go," I said, giving him a quiet tap with my elbow.

He didn't budge, didn't respond at all. Then he turned and walked directly into the rain. He moved quickly enough to be around the corner of the building before Mom saw him. I never called out for him. I knew he'd made up his mind and one conflict was enough for him today.

Mom pulled up to the curb and I rushed to the car before getting soaked. By the time I shut the door, Patrick was out of sight.

I never said anything to her about what happened. Patrick's side of the story would never be taken over a teacher's. I figured he'd been punished enough.

Patrick was suspended ten days for assaulting a teacher. The principal said they considered expulsion, but they decided to be lenient. I'd seen countless times where Patrick sought to make someone miserable. That day was different.

I knew he hated school, and most of the teachers, but I saw something new in his reaction that afternoon. It wasn't that Mr. Biner antagonized him. It was something else.

It was the way he reacted when he had to go home early.

He hated school and made no secret of it. But did he despise being home just as much?

I don't know. I have no idea where he felt like he belonged. That afternoon proved one thing, though.

He was more comfortable walking into a thunderstorm than being in either one of those places.

*CHAPTER 8

You may hear things you didn't expect.

I've been holding the same cup of water for twenty minutes. I'm afraid to put it down. It's been my excuse. When the disposable cup with pink flowers around the middle hits the trash can, I'll be out of distractions from what I've put off all day.

It's time. No one is standing near the casket.

I need to say good-bye to my cousin.

Throughout the wake, I've heard the phrase "Pay my respects" uttered numerous times. No one ever respected Patrick, so I don't get why they're saying they do now.

I've paid attention to exactly what this "paying respects" looks like. Everyone seems to be in on some secret at this wake that I don't know about. People in the procession line have enacted the same ritual over and over.

1. Stand at the coffin.
2. Bow your head.
3. Kneel.
4. Wait ten seconds.
5. Rise and walk toward the back (some do the sign of the cross at this point, but I'm not sure what determines who gets to do that).

I'm good through number three. The rest is still fuzzy to me. I saw a few people talking to themselves while they were kneeling. I think they were saying the Lord's Prayer. Malcolm Somner told me once that being Catholic basically means you memorize two prayers that fit any circumstance. "You need help, want out of trouble, or are thanking God for something? . . . Both work and they are always in a Catholic's back pocket," he would say. Our Easter/Christmas visits to church weren't enough for me to know any prayers. Wish I knew one now, because I have no idea what it means to pay my respects.

I drop the cup into the tiny trash can and head toward Patrick, keeping my eyes locked on his picture instead of him. The lights above the casket seem so much brighter than when we first walked in.

I arrive at the kneeling board (I'm sure there's a fancy religious name for it) and lower myself carefully to not pop the button on my pants. My elbows rest on the dark wooden frame. I try to not look at him, but Patrick's expressionless profile is now directly in front of me.

I hate praying. I feel awkward every time I have to do it. Doesn't matter if it's at church or when Uncle Mike says grace, I never feel right doing it. Almost like God knows I don't feel comfortable praying, and pretending is just lying, and that's even worse.

I can't pretend now. I raise my head and look at Patrick's picture sitting next to the coffin.

That kid despised having his picture taken. *Hate* isn't a strong enough word. It was more like a staged, aggressive protest anytime he knew someone wanted his picture. He would do anything to ruin it. A common scene at family gatherings was my aunt scolding Patrick about his hair/shirt/smile or any other way he was attempting to sabotage the shot. It wasn't like he got a thrill out of it. He truly hated his picture being taken. Maybe there weren't many moments he wanted captured. I'm not sure, but I am a thousand percent positive that having his school picture placed next to his casket wouldn't have been his choice.

I'm not going to speak out loud. I'm just going to say something nice in my head and hope he hears it. I can't kid myself. I'm not kneeling here for him; it's for me. I'll swim with guilt if I don't do this now. There. That's honest, at least.

Patrick, I wish . . . I wish you didn't die. I'm sorry you did. I wish you could see how many people are here right now. And they're really sad. People you thought didn't like you — all here for you. There were times when I wasn't —

I hate this. Is everyone watching me? Feels like everyone has stopped talking and is waiting to see what I do now.

My neck crooks slightly to glance around the room. Not one person is even facing my direction.

Times when I wasn't a good friend to you. I'm sorry for that. I'm sorry that . . . that you died.

That was horrible.

Oh, wow, that was bad.

I need to move.

I stand up trying to remember the last steps of this process and decide to just walk away before anyone sees me. I did it, though. I said good-bye to my dead cousin, who was inches from my face.

No one is looking at me like I thought. Maybe no one even noticed I was kneeling in front of Patrick. Maybe tomorrow will be the same and no one will notice my speech, either.

The crowd is finally winding down. The room has cleared out to where you can see more of the walls. Just random clusters of people now, instead of the line that took over the room. No one is crying anymore, just talking.

Aunt Millie has someone else's hand. I bet she's held thirty by now. My parents are with a man and woman in the corner and have their concerned faces on while nodding politely. The woman is pointing to her knee and making a face like she stepped on a Lego.

Wait . . .

Legos. Patrick loved Legos! That's actually not a horrible memory!

I could totally make that into a kind-of sort-of nice speech about Patrick. In grade school, he loved getting new sets and building things in his room. I could easily talk about that for two minutes. I need to write this down. I'll start with —

Wait. Where is it?

My paper. Where did it go? It was just in my pocket a minute ago and —

My sport coat. I must have left it in my sport-coat pocket. My sport coat that is staring at me from across the room, underneath Sofia's sleeping head. That's what I get for not telling Aunt Rose where her bracelet was.

All right. Not a massive emergency. I still have the pen, just need another piece of paper. I'll rip another one from the book and start writing again. It's not like I have a ton written down anyway. I'll make my way to the guest book, do another fake cough, and sneak another page out.

A man and woman I don't recognize are at the guest book. But . . . they aren't signing it. They're reading it? Can you do that? I'm not close enough to hear them, but I can tell they are going through each name, as if they are checking a team roster. I thought the book was just for the family to see who came, not for the nosy guests.

I need a piece of paper. I have to write this down. I haven't had a single idea today and I'm not about to lose this one before someone grabs me and makes me talk to them. Where can I find some paper?

The guest book is a lost cause. Those people are locked into their judging of who came and who didn't. I don't see them walking away from their job anytime soon.

All right. No paper lying around, and the book is not an option. Why is a simple thing like a piece of paper so hard to find when you need it? There has to be one piece somewhere tha —

The scrapbook. The one Aunt Rose brought.

Patrick's collection of schoolwork, letters to Santa, and various other memories. All on paper.

It's still closed. I bet no one even looked in it today. I'm sure I could "borrow" one page from it and he wouldn't care. He probably was forced to write everything in there anyway. He won't miss it if I take just one piece. Besides, I can return it. I'm just going to use the back of something anyway.

I can do this. The key is to appear very interested in looking at Patrick's scrapbook, and not like I'm about to steal something from him at his own wake. I'll flip it open, skim a few pages, and very quietly remove something from the plastic liner.

So far, so good. No one has approached me; no one has noticed me. I'm one with my surroundings. I'll flip through the book a little more until I find anything that has blank space.

Pictures he drew in kindergarten?

No.

Old birthday party invitation?

No.

Patrick's "Letter to the President" assignment from civics last year? Hold on — this may do.

I remember this. We each had to pick a topic that was important to us and write to the president. Mr. Hernandez made copies of all our letters and mailed them himself. I remember Patrick was pretty excited at the thought of the president reading his letter on child soldiers in Africa. I was more realistic and figured they were never even sent.

The front of the letter was perfectly typed in 12-point font, contained no mistakes, and had an *Outstanding job!* scribbled in red pen at the top. His letter was three paragraphs long and signed at the bottom.

Which meant the back would be a gloriously blank slate for me to write my speech on.

Don't even look to see if anyone is watching. Commit

to getting this piece of paper and get to the bathroom. Move away from everyone and get this speech down.

I fold the paper twice, stuff it into my pocket, and make my way to the bathroom. Once in the locked stall, I'll have at least ten minutes alone to finally get this speech written.

I'm on a mission. If anyone talks to me, I'll ignore them and keep moving. I can't handle thinking about this speech any longer and need to get this written down before I forget it.

The bathroom is empty. The stall is mine. The door lock clicks.

All right, where to start? *Patrick and his Legos. He could build anything out of them.* That's a good start, nice, not made up, no horrible episodes.

The pen finds its way out of my pocket as I unfold his civics assignment. Patrick never got a lot of positive feedback from teachers. I can see why Aunt Rose picked this for the scrapbook. When he was excited about an assignment, he could actually knock it out of the park. Then there was the other ninety-nine percent of assignments that he struck out on.

Time to hammer this thing out. I could talk about the space station he spent a week making and wouldn't let anyone come near. And the city he built that was supposed to be from the last empir—

Wait.

What's this?

The paper rests unfolded between my hands. Patrick's A+ letter to the president on one side, but the back is anything but blank.

It's Patrick's handwriting. Only much, much sloppier. Penmanship was never a strength of his, but this looks like he wrote it in a hurry. On a moving train. During a hurricane. I can barely make out what it says.

Mr President
  I dont know if u care at all cuz you should care about things like this cuz they happen and its not fair to some of the people in it. Many reasons at least 3 countries in Africa do this and will self destruct if they keep going with the cruel ways and no one is doing anything about them to help them or anything for them. this makes 2 times i have written to do something while the world will ignore all of them before

they have no time and its not fair. If I could do just 1 thing to help and make this better for them you should do the same thing for them too cuz there is no time and they have no help so you should help them cuz no one is doing anything for them at all and it doesnt make any sense why people dont see there is NO WAY OUt for them.

It's Patrick. He must have written this after he got the assignment back. I flip to the front side: the typed, articulate, organized side with a compliment in red ink. And back again to Patrick's scattered, jumbled voice.

It doesn't make any sense. It's all over the place. I know his brain worked fast at times, but I've never seen it in writing like this. Is this how he always thought about stuff? All . . . whatever this is? I don't know how his hands kept up with his thoughts, or if they did at all.

I read it again, looking for some sense in it. I'm only more lost.

I don't get it. How can these be written by the same

person? How can I have known Patrick all of my life and still be so confused about who he was?

I don't know if I can make sense of this note. I don't even know who it was written for or why. The more I think about him, the less I understand. Patrick never said anything was wrong, though. He never said anything about why he acted the way he did.

But things like this note . . .

Was Patrick trying to say something?

"Why don't you and Patrick go play outside?"

That was one of my least favorite questions from Mom because it was a command in disguise. My face always reflected my feelings about that idea no matter how hard I tried to hide it.

"How 'bout we just stay in?"

I knew Mom wanted an escape from him as much as I did. Usually we had Sofia as a buffer, but she was at her school for a fund-raiser. I feared Patrick would be my responsibility for the afternoon.

"Jimmy . . ."

"Why don't we just stay here and cook something

instead?" I responded without looking away from the TV. She knew Patrick and sharp kitchen objects would be disastrous.

I got the glare. The one she thought Patrick didn't notice.

"Maybe we could even cook something up on the grill." Adding fire to the mix only made her more assertive that we go outside and do something. I knew this but said it anyway.

"Nope. You two need to get out. Too nice a day."

"It's freezing. We can't be out in this bitter cold."

"It's April. It's not freezing. Put on a sweatshirt and go."

"Go where?"

"You're twelve. You two can find something to do on your own."

"Like wha—?"

"Go." A one-word response meant the discussion was over.

Patrick stood up and muttered something about an idea. That's the second phrase I didn't like to hear.

He led the way as we walked out the back door. Our yard isn't very big, at least not big enough for whatever Patrick had in mind. He went through the space between two lilac bushes and through the Petersons' yard.

"Where we going?"

No response. Patrick had become quieter lately and didn't tell anyone anything he didn't have to. He gave me a look that meant one of two things: something was going to get smashed or blown up.

The town of Harper is laid out like most small towns I've seen. The downtown area has the usual bank, library, diner, and a few other small shops. While there are tracks running through the area, Harper isn't big enough to get its own stop. It isn't like we ever took the train much anyway. The nearest depot is about three miles west, in the neighboring town of Kingsley. It has a pool, a theater, and restaurants with cloth napkins. A solid stretch of woods separates us from our more affluent neighbor. Harper was commonly known as "poor man's Kingsley."

One of Patrick's favorite things to do was follow the tracks that separate the towns into the woods. Not so much to go to Kingsley, just into the woods. It was quiet and possibly dangerous all at the same time, just like Patrick.

I knew we were headed into the woods before he

even said a word. He'd always loved following the tracks, especially when we were younger and not allowed to do it. That made it even more appealing to him. Now his parents didn't care if we walked them.

Every year since kindergarten, we ventured a little farther into the woods. As six-year-olds, we never left the view of the Harper crossing. By fourth grade, we were well out of range of anyone's voice in Harper. Since then we had walked clear to Kingsley several times, but usually we stopped halfway. There was something about not seeing where the tracks ended that appealed to both of us. We never shared this out loud. We just knew it.

The forest was thickest in the middle between the two towns. This was where we'd always come to build forts. It was the one time I enjoyed Patrick's company. I liked to build the most creative and functional fort, while Patrick preferred to build the deadliest traps around it. It wasn't as if international warlords were trying to find our fort and take it over, but he liked to prepare for the worst. Once he built a Burmese tiger trap in front of my lean-to design. For a week after that, I dreaded hearing about the wrongful death of someone's dog and had my "It was all Patrick's idea" speech ready just in case. Never happened, thankfully.

We hadn't built a fort in a couple of years, so it couldn't be that. I also knew he didn't want to walk all the way to Kingsley. I asked again and got the same "smashed or blown-up" look.

We arrived at the usual midway spot, and Patrick started digging in his sweatshirt pockets. He fished out an assortment of change, a key, a couple of fishing weights, and tape.

"Always wanted to make railroad art," he said while placing the items on a stump. Smashing it is.

"Let's see what happens to these on the tracks. I heard they go totally flat," Patrick said, squinting slightly at the objects. I admit I was curious to see what would happen. He kept his eyes fixed on the items the way a mechanic looks at a stalled engine. "Two-thirty train should be coming soon. Let's see how the key does."

Patrick got down on one knee and surveyed the line of track in front of him. He ran one hand down the top, looking for the optimal place for the key to spend its final minutes in its current form.

"This should do," he muttered to himself while placing the key on the track.

"What is that a key to?" I asked.

221

"Not sure. Found it in our junk drawer."

"You don't know if it's important? Or if it's the only copy?"

"If it were important, it wouldn't be in a junk drawer." I could never understand Patrick's logic. But I couldn't quite argue with it, either.

We both stood up as the sound of the Harper crossing bell echoed toward us.

"Here it comes. Let's see what the weights look like, too." We still had some time before the train rumbled through. Patrick grabbed three of the fishing weights and taped them onto the track just to the left of the key. "Not sure if those will stay, but it's worth a shot."

He walked back to the stump. We could see the train coming. Still had about thirty seconds.

"And now, my apologies, Mr. President, but I want to see what you look like with a fat face," Patrick declared, grabbing one of the pennies. He walked to the track, looking for the ideal place for the experiment.

"Hey . . . hurry up! Train's almost here," I said, trying to mask my excitement. Still feeling the track for Mr. Lincoln's spot, he ignored me until finding the perfect place for his artwork. He walked back to the stump, never once glancing at the oncoming train.

We stood on either side of the stump with what remained of the unscathed metal between us. The train was about one hundred yards away and getting bigger by the second.

In all the times I had been in these woods with Patrick, I always did my best to hide my fear of a train being so close to us when it roared by. When you're at home or anywhere in town you can hear it. You can see it from anywhere downtown, and it's something that always commands respect. But seeing the train from a distance is tremendously different from being five feet away when it passes by. You don't realize how big an engine is until you're in spitting distance from its size and power. Its massive sound is deafening. I would always grind my teeth to hide my anxiety when it stormed by us. Patrick always studied it as if he were admiring an exhibit at a museum. It would roar by while he stood unflinching, motionless, and asking some question in his head only he knew.

We kept our eyes focused on the metal objects as the mighty wheels approached, but we lost sight of them after the first car passed by. We couldn't tell if our creations had been taken for a ride or were pushed between the rails. Patrick took a step closer as the cars barreled past us. I stayed back, planted firmly in my spot. He inched forward even farther, searching for any remnants, not once looking at the massive railcars flying by. He was an arm's length away from the train now. My teeth hurt.

"Patrick!" No use. He couldn't hear me. Even if he could, it wouldn't matter. He was kneeling down now, scanning for any trace of what we left for the train to reconfigure. If there were anything sticking out of the side of the train, it surely would have taken his head off. Thankfully, it was a commuter train and passed quickly with only a few cars.

Patrick leaned his head forward in harmony with the end of the last car to inspect the outcome. From my angle, it looked as though his face were going to be removed. While my teeth were nearly ground out of my jaw, Patrick couldn't have looked more at peace.

"Nicely done," he boasted. He held up the key, which no longer resembled a key. It wasn't perfectly flat, as I had hoped, but any chance of the key regaining its former self was gone.

"Here's one of the weights." He picked up what now

looked like a bad nickel. This result was disappointing. Fishing weights don't have much shape to begin with, so I don't know what I expected. "Where's the penny? I want to see Lincoln's fat face."

Patrick looked up and down the side of the rail and found the penny facedown on the wooden tie. "Nope, fell off." He picked it up and looked at it as if it were going to tell him something. "Tape isn't strong enough. Maybe if we placed it somewhere else . . ."

Patrick saw this as a defeat, and he didn't accept defeat well. I actually wanted to see what would happen to the penny, too. "We need to try again," he said. "There's a freight that usually comes around three."

"How do you know that?"

"Just do."

This was how Patrick operated. He had so many teachers convinced that he was lazy. When he had a goal, he did his homework and was well prepared.

I knew my mom wouldn't care if we were out later than expected. I reached over to the stump and grabbed a penny of my own. I wanted to see this happen, too.

"OK," I chimed in. "Let's look for a better spot. What if each of us tapes one on a different rail, and then see if one of them stays?"

We didn't stray far from the stump at first, but then we walked down the tracks a bit more. Both of us walked with a rail between our feet, scouring it for any kind of indentation that would better hold a penny in place to meet its demise. Patrick took a quiet knee. He'd found a spot.

While he examined the rail and how the penny would stay, I surveyed the rest of the setting. The thick of the forest was much closer to the tracks now. "I think we'll be too close to the train here. Let's go back."

Patrick was on both knees, rotating the penny in its spot.

"Then go."

He was committed. The anxiety of being close to the train passing had now been outweighed by my curiosity. I sucked it up and searched out a place for Mr. Lincoln on the rail parallel to Patrick's.

He was putting the finishing touches on his placement while quietly stating, "This time . . . you won't be so lucky, Mr. President." We both stood up as the familiar whistle sounded.

Three o'clock. Patrick was right.

He took a few steps to the side and squatted down to view the arrangement. I moved toward him, stepping over his rail, careful not to disturb his surgical setup. Being on the far side of my rail, I wasn't going to see my penny get squished. That was fine. I just wanted this train to pass and hoped it was a short one.

We could see the engine approaching. The earth started to tremble as it always does when you're this close to an unstoppable force. We watched our respective pennies and would find out in the next twenty seconds if we were going to be successful. The tiny stones between the wooden ties began to shake. Patrick's eyes stayed fixed on his penny, and I hoped he'd stay next to me this time. When I saw it happen, I knew he wouldn't.

While his stayed put, mine fell off, a victim to the vibrations that ran through the rails, reminding us of what was coming. I'd hoped he didn't see it. I looked toward the engine fast approaching, at least fast enough for me to take a step back into the tree that stopped me. I grabbed a branch at my side like it was a fence holding me back from a cliff.

By the time I looked away from the branch I was gripping, Patrick was stepping over his penny toward mine. It got loud: metal-wheels-on-metal-rails loud. The engine horn blasted twice — somehow loud enough to outcry the machine — and only added to my panic. It was close enough to hit with a baseball.

"Patrick!" No good. He was across and bending toward my penny.

"Patrick! Stop!" He was going to get hit. Or at least lose his arm. I didn't want to see either. I didn't want to be here. My hands were moving, circling without my control.

"MOVE!"

I have no doubt it was the loudest I yelled in my life. He was setting the penny down, looking steadily at the rail as if unaware a train was about to collide with him like a mosquito on a windshield.

"PATRI —"

The engine passed in a gust of wind. I frantically looked to the other side for any sign of my cousin, only to have my view blocked by the passing cars.

Nothing.

A split second between passing cars.

Again, nothing.

Another snapshot of time and no cousin standing on the other side.

More snapshots.

Nothing.

The train had taken him.

I looked toward Harper, where the engine came from, hoping to see the end car. Freight train, no chance. The cars were infinite. Why? It was a stupid penny! Why did he care? He was gone over a penny! I gripped my safety branch even tighter, hoping the mechanical beast would pass.

I looked straight ahead through a blurred space between cars.

It couldn't be.

Looked like Patrick's head.

Another blur.

It was.

It was Patrick.

Crouching down and focused on the rail was my cousin. Alive. Every other second gave me a glimpse across the tracks, reassuring me he was all right. He stared transfixed near where the pennies were placed. I turned my head toward Harper again to see that this train was mortal, and its caboose approached.

When the last car passed, I loosened my grip on the branch. Patrick never even looked at me. I'm not even sure he heard me shouting at him . . . or cared. He waited for the clearing and reached toward the rails. I said nothing. Just watched him carefully pick up two completely flattened pieces of copper and examine them in his hand.

"You can still see his eyes on yours. Check out his hair," he said, passing my newly flattened penny over. I released the branch and stepped toward him. He stood with one foot on the ground and one on the rail, the way a hunter stands over an animal he's shot. He extended the penny toward me while examining his own. "I should have cleaned mine first. Face would've come out better."

I took my penny and pretended to examine it, but I still couldn't see anything except the train ending my cousin. I composed myself enough to say, "Let's head back." He didn't respond at first. He just stared at his penny for a moment before tossing it into the woods.

"Don't you want to keep it?"

"Dad would be pissed if he knew I did that. Not worth it. Let's go."

No words were shared the entire walk home. I had no idea what to say. I don't think Patrick had many thoughts he felt like sharing.

I didn't understand why my cousin was willing to

risk his life like that. For a penny. Then throw it away?

Patrick came within a few inches of death yet stood there calmly.

Maybe he didn't notice he could have died.

Maybe he didn't care.

*CHAPTER 9

If you're not sure what to say about the deceased, don't share your thoughts.

I survey the remaining mourners. Only about a dozen people left. They all have their coats on, even Aunt Millie. This must be the end. As glad as I am that the wake is almost over, it only means the funeral and my speech are getting closer.

I can't do this speech tomorrow.

I can't.

My parents are talking to someone from Uncle Mike's work. As soon as they leave, I'll ask them — no, beg them — to have someone else speak.

I make my way to the oversize chairs. Sofia is in one of them, curled up like a cat and still asleep with

Norman under her arm. I take over the other one and wait for my parents to find us.

Their friends leave, Aunt Millie leaves, and so do the rest of the guests.

"You guys head home," Dad tells Uncle Mike. "I'll take care of everything here and see you in the morning."

Uncle Mike doesn't argue as he carefully scoops Sofia from her spot without waking her. They thank my parents and hug me before leaving.

"I'm going to tell Marty that everyone's cleared out and just make sure we're set for tomorrow. Be back in a second."

Mom and I stand at the poster boards of Patrick's pictures. Even though she spent most of yesterday afternoon putting these together, I haven't looked at them until now.

"Remember this?" she asks, pointing to a frame of my seventh birthday, where Patrick was hovering over my chocolate cake.

"Uh-huh." I remember it well. That was when I got a squirt gun from Uncle Mike. It lasted ten minutes. Patrick broke it. I never even got to use it. I was still crying when I blew out my candles.

"You were so mad at him," Mom says quietly, and smiles.

"Mom?"

Deep breath.

"Mom, I don't want to give the speech tomorrow."

She hasn't taken her eyes off the birthday picture. She responds in the exact same manner she did earlier. "You'll be fine."

She doesn't hear me.

"Mom, please. Please don't make me. I hate talking in front of people." My voice is shaking. Mom turns from the picture of my birthday and is now focusing on a different one of us at Halloween, before Sofia was born.

"No one likes it, but you have to do it. For your aunt and uncle. You're Patrick's only cousin and that means a lot to them. You'll be fine." Her voice is calm. She focuses on another picture. "Remember this? You were such a funny cowboy. . . ."

She still doesn't hear me.

I'm losing control of my voice. "Mom, please. I don't even know what to say. I don't know what to say at all."

She breaks from the pictures.

"James."

Nothing good happens after my formal name is used.

"You need to do this for your aunt, your uncle, Sofia, and most of all for Patrick. We don't get to choose everything we want to do in life. You think Aunt Rose wants to be here now? You think she is choosing to bury her son?"

I'm tired. I'm scared. My waist hurts. Words are just coming out.

"I don't care about that. I don't want to do it. Please don't make me stand up in front of everyone. Patrick was never even nice to me! What am I supposed to say about someone who was never nice to me?"

"Enough! None of us wants to be here, but we have to!" The anger in her voice escalates quickly. "Your cousin died, James. And this is what we have to do."

"I know, but —" My words can't catch up with my tears. Anxiety about public speaking, a cousin dying, and no one listening all boils out of me.

"Your aunt wants you to pay your respects to him tomorrow, and that is what you need to do. Your cousin died and it's awful. He didn't —"

"I know, but, Mom —"

"He made a poor choice and this is the result."

Why? Why won't she listen to me?

"But, Mom, I —"

"He shouldn't have gone out on the ice and —"

"I know, but —"

"He shouldn't have been wearing hockey skates —"

"But I —"

"Not on the pond — he should have known better."

I'm sniffling in that uncontrollable way that makes it harder to talk.

"Jimmy, your aunt has been through enough and we need to help her thro —"

"I don't care!"

She stops. I have her attention, but now I don't think I want it.

"Jimmy, how could you say someth —?"

"And why don't you protect me like you protect her?" I'm louder now, maybe yelling. The words are just spilling out.

"Enough. That is *not* true and not —"

"It is true! You're always worried about her and never me! You always pick her ov —"

"Stop. Now." Her hand grips my arm, the part everyone keeps rubbing. It momentarily stops my word

236

flood. "None of us are happy to be here. None of us chose it. This is what we have to do for each other."

I do my best to find a breath before speaking. Her hand remains clamped on my arm. This is it. A last-ditch effort of appeal. No smart-mouthed comment, no banter — just a sincere plea for help.

"Mom, please. I don't want to talk about Patrick tomorrow."

Her grip only tightens.

"We don't always get to choose what we want to do and —"

"But that's just it, Mom!"

"Just it what?"

Here goes. . . .

"What if Patrick . . . ?"

"What?"

"What if it wasn't an accident?"

No response.

Not even a blink.

The words are in control now. "What if he didn't care if he —?"

"What? If he what?"

"If he drowned."

Only now do I realize that I haven't once said the

word *drowned* since Patrick died. Hearing myself say it brings the tears on full force.

"That doesn't make any sense. Why would he not care?"

"No . . . I'm not saying that. . . . I don't mean that he . . ." I'm losing control.

"Then what? What are you saying?"

"I'm saying what if he knew this would happen? What if he chose to go out on the ice and knew he wouldn't come back?"

So many firsts have come into my life during this week of Patrick's death.

I've never been to a wake before.

I've never seen a dead body before.

I've never been slapped by my mother before.

I don't even see her hand move, much less her arm. I certainly feel it, though. All five fingers and her grandma's birthstone ring . . . I feel each one of them strike with force across my cheek. Dad spanked me more than once when I was little, but I've never been slapped. It doesn't hurt as bad as getting spanked, but the shock of getting hit in the face serves its own purpose.

Mom doesn't say a word. She turns back to the pictures and finds a new one to focus on. I have no idea how getting a stinger like that didn't make me cry more, but it smacked the tears right out of me. We stand there silently, not sure what else to do. Mom looks at the pictures; I look at anything but her. With my back to the door, I hear Dad return to the parlor as he's putting on his coat.

"Everything's taken care of for tomorrow, so we can leave. All set?" His voice matches his eyes, showing the wear of all the interactions today brought.

Mom barely looks at me as she turns toward him. "All set. Get your coat, Jimmy." Her voice is as casual as if we were going to the movies.

She didn't want me to interfere. The family law.

It's settled.

I'll be speaking at my cousin's funeral tomorrow.

I don't want to do it. I hate being forced to do things in front of people.

That's another thing I always had in common with Patrick.

The summer before eighth grade was my introduction to marching-band culture. The high school offered a one-week camp that included the junior-high musicians.

We learned the basics of marching band and worked on a halftime routine that would be performed at the football season opener. To the parents, it was sold as a "fantastic connection to high-school marching band." To us, more like boot camp.

We were informed within three minutes of the first day that we were probies (probationary members) and this was a tryout. We knew that wasn't true, but it seemed to be a hazing tradition. Even though all of us had performed in parades in junior-high band, the high-school players let us know that we hadn't even been born yet. The week was spent partly in the band room, learning the music, and partly on the field, learning formations for the halftime show. The last day included an evening dress rehearsal for all those performing, grades seven through twelve.

If you weren't in band, seeing the musicians get ready for a performance looked like some perverse group ritual that was a lawsuit waiting to happen. Getting dressed as a group is part of the culture. All fifty-seven of us in the band room, guys and girls alike, changed into our uniforms together for the dress rehearsal performance.

I really didn't understand why all band uniforms were ugly and uncomfortable. Modeling a horrific blend of dark orange and black, the Harper High School Marching Band attire was no exception to that rule. The tops were cardboard-like and almost unbendable. No part of them moved efficiently enough so that an instrument could be played well. Never in my life did I think I'd be changing clothes in front of this many people, wearing shoulder tassels, or slipping on polyester pants, yet there I was.

The pants were actually kind of amazing, though. Each pair was created to fit every person in the room, no matter their size. The material was cheap and itchy and reminded me of old curtains, but the design was genius. Inside the waist was a series of intricate buckles and bands of elastic. All you needed to do was pull them up, tighten the bands, then fasten the buckles. Presto! Pants that fit.

I learned quickly that despite being one band, specific instrument players stuck together and embraced how different they were from every other member of the band. The individual groups had one thing in common, though: they each felt they were the most vital piece of the band. They had their own personality, and nothing brought that out more than how each dressed before performing.

The flutes — an all-female section that smiled politely and followed directions better than anyone — took the far corner. The other groups liked to tease them for it, but the flutes seemed to almost like it. They all wore T-shirts, so nothing was exposed, but shorts that showed off enough leg to garner attention from the males.

Next to them was the other all-girl section: the clarinets. Another group of rule-followers, but they weren't really teased, more ignored. Two of them had messy hair, one had glasses bigger than her face, and a fourth never looked anyone in the eye. No one in the room seemed more uncomfortable with this "group dressing room" concept than the clarinets.

The trombones took over the far side of the room. An all-male section with their own code. No group seemed to enjoy band more than the trombones. A day of rehearsal did not happen without the word "tromboner" blurted out at least four times. When the baton went up, though, these guys were all business. They wore the uniform with pride.

The trumpet section was another male-heavy group, but one that felt they were legends in all aspects of band. And life in general. The group was weirdly confident and obnoxiously loud. They made every effort for the flutes to see them change clothes.

My section was in the back corner. We were a mixed breed: six guys and two girls. Each of us changed with the full support of concealing clothing already in place as we slipped into our polyester wardrobe. Our section looked out for one another, knowing the rest of the band saw us as harmony rather than melody. We were the reliable bandmates, the shoulders to cry on, the moral compass of the group; we were the saxophones.

On the top riser, a step above all others, was the loudest group — the percussion section. The drums felt they were above everyone else and frequently reminded others that they determined the tempo of a performance. During parades, games, and pep rallies, the percussion section was the only group that played alone while the rest of the band waited patiently.

The crowd always responded to the drumline, and the percussionists knew it. That's where they came alive, banging away with passion and purpose. Sometimes they went off script and did their own little number that none of us knew was coming. Sometimes they changed the tempo just because they could.

It was one of the few places Patrick fit right in.

Unlike me, Patrick had no issue with getting dressed in front of others. Anytime we went to the pool, I turned around to take off my shirt and raced to immerse myself in the water. I was always envious of Patrick's confidence. He didn't care what others thought and had no fear of how he looked with his shirt off. Maybe it was more ignorance than confidence, but I was jealous either way. As I looked toward the drums, I saw my cousin: bare-chested and sitting down, taking his sweet time to get his top organized before putting it on.

"Warm-ups! Two minutes!" came the warning bellow from the senior drum major, Jack Rossi.

This dress rehearsal, these performances, this moment — this was what Jack Rossi lived for. Not a big guy for a senior, nor did he have a commanding presence as a leader. As drum major, though, he was in charge for the evening. In the junior-high band, the teacher led the class (like any other class). In this high-school mini-camp, the drum major led almost everything. The junior-high members were given that directive during the welcome comments of day one.

The orders came the way a drill sergeant would give them to new recruits. The high-school players always referred to him by his full name, never just "Jack" or "Rossi." He seemed to embrace this and grinned at the music that was the sound of his own name.

"Anyone not set in two minutes —" he echoed from the door, making sure to pause for effect. I learned quickly that he liked to stay by the door as long as possible. Jack Rossi liked to make an entrance. When he wasn't around, we referred to him as Jack Russell for his similarities to the terrier breed. But no one called him that to his face. His temper was the major reason he earned that nickname.

"Gets wall sits."

Jack Rossi loved giving out his wall sits, and somehow they were enforced by the rest of the band. An acceptable form of corporal punishment, a wall sit meant putting your back against the wall, dropping your knees to ninety degrees, and holding that pose for a designated amount of time. It doesn't sound bad, but it's excruciating. Jack Rossi had a creepy half smile whenever he dished them out, particularly when he saw fear in the junior-high musicians. He was one of those guys who make you wonder how he's gotten this far in life without someone giving him a severe beating.

The shuffling in the room picked up, and within

two minutes, we'd somehow all be prepared for warm-ups. I raced to tie my shoes and straighten my jacket. When I opened my case, I noticed him.

Patrick.

He hadn't moved. He was still sitting hunched over with his shirt off. The room was peppered with orange-and-black formalwear, and here was this shirtless kid staring at the kettledrum before him.

"Patrick. Patrick! Hey!" I whisper-shouted to get his attention.

Nothing.

Oh, no. I knew where this was going. The other percussionists saw him but were ignoring the problem in their section. I hopped over to his riser.

"Patrick, get ready! You're going to have to do wall sits!"

He pulled in a labored breath. He didn't look up, but he did move and start to put his shirt and jacket on.

"One minute! The wall is lonely!" Jack Rossi shouted again.

"Patrick, come on! Get your shoes on. You still need to button up, get the sti —"

He stood up, straight up. Right in my face. He didn't

look mad, though. More . . . tired. He also didn't look eager for help. I backed away and returned to my seat.

Patrick buttoned his coat and slipped the shoes on his feet without tying them. He ran his fingers through his unkempt hair and gripped his mallets. A little disheveled, but at a glance, he'd pass inspection.

"Warm-ups!" bellowed Jack Rossi from the side entrance.

While the word we heard was "warm-ups," the words Jack Rossi heard in his head were "This is my moment, people!" It was time. His time.

The room fell silent and the terrier approached his musicians. Jack Rossi stepped with a casual stride, taking in the quiet power he commanded over the room. He ascended his podium and surveyed his subordinates. Even on the podium, he was still a small guy. Satisfied with what he saw, he raised the baton.

"Exercise three. Hold the long notes. Wait for my 'cue."

Jack Rossi raised the baton and the band followed orders by setting reeds to lips and sticks to rims. He moved his hand, ever so slightly, and the music happened. Jack Rossi seemed to conserve the amount of movement he used in each of these starting motions, almost as if he were seeing how much he could control the band with so little effort.

Every section did its part to sound as one unit, while Jack Rossi eyeballed each of us to let us know he was there.

The baton swung sideways. We stopped as commanded.

Jack Rossi ceased scanning the room and focused on someone.

"Probie. Shoelaces. Two shoes equals two minutes on the wall."

Oh, no, no, no . . .

Patrick was standing far enough away from the kettledrum that it wasn't hiding his feet. He stood with his shoulders slumped and eyes glazed. He didn't respond. I didn't know if he was aware the entire band had stopped playing because of him.

"Probie! I'm talking to you! We perform in thirty minutes, and you just wasted two by not being ready. Get to the wall."

Oh, I hoped and wished and prayed that Patrick would just get in position on the wall before this got worse.

"The entire band is waiting for you to find the wall. Move it!"

A frustrated groan and head shake came from the musicians, none more profound than those from Patrick's own section. He looked to the wall by the side entrance.

And stared.

I had no idea what he was thinking or what decision he was processing, but this was new. This was typically where Patrick lost control verbally. And emotionally. And physically. He kept staring. He was winding up for something much worse.

"Make that three minutes for still wasting our time! Move it!"

I wished this short excuse of a leader would stop barking. *He has no idea how my cousin will haul off on the world if he keeps pushing.* He raised the baton again, daring any of us to be out of line.

"Anyone else not ready?"

Jack Rossi wanted another target. The band focused on the baton, careful not to look directly at the mad dog. Patrick still hadn't moved.

"B-flat scale, staccato, legato, then hold two—"

That son of a bi—

"—and separate two continually."

He threw out an advanced jazz band warm-up. We didn't know it. He wanted to make an example of someone else. The baton scooped, and again, the music happened.

Patrick moved.

His hand relaxed first. The mallets fell to the floor. It reminded me of a movie I'd seen where a lady shot a guy and her hand just let the gun fall. He took another breath, just like the one I saw before. Labored and difficult. He stepped off the riser and plowed into the horns section.

This was it. Jack Rossi had no idea the public display of anger he was about to be dragged into.

The baton stopped. So did the music.

"What is your problem? You ever want to play in my band again, you'll get on the wall!"

Patrick was going to assault the small senior at the front of the room. I knew in two seconds that this tiny man of a drum major would be thrown against the floor and his punishment would only have begun. I didn't know if anyone would stop it, either. I didn't think I could do it myself.

Patrick was off the risers now, a few feet in front of the podium.

Here comes the hurt. . . .

But it didn't come.

Patrick walked to the wall. We all watched in horrified silence as my cousin took weighted step after step toward it. I'd seen Patrick in numerous conflicts, but never like this. Never so . . . tired.

"Make that four minutes now, probie!"

His eyes looked different. Not full of rage, not teary, not anything. The light was gone out of them. He stepped forward until his back was to me.

Patrick wasn't walking to the wall for his consequence.

He was leaving.

Ignoring the condescending voice screaming commands at him, he walked straight to the exit and through the doors.

They shut loudly behind him, like a downbeat. We all looked back at Jack Rossi, now swollen and red. His shoulders moved hurriedly up and down with his breath. We could have kept time off them. He was embarrassed in front of his own band.

During his moment.

By a probie.

"We don't need him. We don't need him for tonight, anyway," he said to himself, but looked at us. "Again." He raised the baton and we followed orders. That's what we were trained to do.

Patrick never returned to band. Not just that night but for the year. Depending on who you asked, the reason varied. Jack Rossi's version was that he threw Patrick out of band permanently. Uncle Mike and Aunt Rose said it was interfering with his grades and he had to quit.

I heard everyone's story. Except Patrick's.

Seeing my cousin challenge authority wasn't anything new, but that night stayed with me. It wasn't his getting in trouble or being yelled at that was the most haunting part. It was what the rest of us did when we saw Patrick's tired eyes.

It was when the music stopped.

And we just sat and watched.

*CHAPTER 10

Everyone has a story — especially the quiet kids.

Back at home, my room is fantastically spacious, with no other bodies or voices. The wake is over, and no one is asking for my attention.

My waistline is slowly recovering from the deformed shape those pants created. At least I can breathe a little before having to put them on again in the morning. Once this speech is written, I can go to bed and not think about it.

All right, what to say about Patrick? Which story can I tell?

Nothing triggers the horrible effects of anxiety like a blank page mixed with a very public deadline.

OK, just get this done. No one is expecting Shakespeare tomorrow, just a few nice words about Patrick. I've written plenty of last-minute papers that sound like I know what I'm talking about. That's what separates us Honors kids from regular English students. We're not any smarter, just better at shoveling it on the page.

Nice story . . . nice story . . .

Didn't get too far with Legos, so what else? The time we all went to the fair was fun. Until he flipped out over not winning the ringtoss and Uncle Mike had to fireman-carry him to the car.

Nope.

Trick-or-treating when we were nine was fun. Until he got in a fight with a little Abe Lincoln over the historical inconsistencies of his costume. Patrick felt that since Lincoln was likely left-handed, he would have never carried his bag of candy with his right hand. Abe's dad didn't appreciate the constructive criticism.

I just want tomorrow over with. Every part of it. I don't want to think about this speech. I don't want to think about the funeral. I don't want to think about Patrick again.

OK, one paragraph. I can do this. I still have Legos

to fall back on, but I don't know if I can get a few minutes out of that one. Let's see. . . . What else did he like? Patrick liked . . . the zoo! There. The zoo. I can talk about the time we went to the zoo and everyone had fun. Until Patrick went into the reptile house and started —

A knock.

A pause.

The door.

Mom.

The absolute last person I want invading my short-lived space.

She comes in, timidly. She knows I'm mad. My cheek still radiates from our last discussion.

"Jimmy?"

I'm not saying a word. I learned my lesson.

"Jimmy, I'd like to talk to you." She sits on the end of my bed. "About something from earlier."

Perfect. Exactly what I want right now is to have a meaningful conversation with the person who just slapped me. This should get my creative pistons firing.

"When you"— she pauses —"asked me about Patrick earlier —"

She's not looking at me. She must have actually realized how mean it was to hit me. I'll let her apologize, then she can leave.

"I reacted in a way I shouldn't have."

Mom sucks at apologies. She'll say everything but "I'm sorry." She's speaking slower than normal, though. Maybe she actually does feel bad.

"I told your father about it, and we agreed I needed to talk to you."

She'll skirt around those two words a little more before convincing herself it's enough, and then hopefully leave.

"I told him I wanted to talk to you alone. Because I . . ."

Let's get this over with.

"I wanted to talk to you."

Got it. You just said that. Why is she acting so weird?

"It caught me by surprise when you asked about your cousin. I . . . I hadn't thought of what happened that way and I —"

She still hasn't looked at me. She usually stares through me when telling me something important. This is new.

"I was very upset and I reacted."

256

Yes, I know. You reacted on my face. Good for you for stating the obvious. I'm really not in the mood for a halfhearted apology. I just want to write something down, go to bed, and forget about everything involving Patrick Feeny's life. And death.

"I..."

Hold on. She still hasn't looked up. She hasn't said sorry but is acting really strange, like I was the one who hit her.

"When you said that about Patrick, it..."

Another long pause.

I sit a little straighter. I'm still mad but very curious.

"It made me think of something that I didn't want to think about." Her head lifts slightly, her eyes straight ahead. "I didn't want to think about Patrick making a choice like that —"

Wait. She's about to cry. She almost never cries.

I sit upright, setting my pad of paper aside. Mom collects herself, just before a tear can flow.

"Because that is —"

She looks at me with something I have never seen on her face before. Fear.

"How my father died."

Holy balls.

I have officially lost track of how many people have rendered me without the use of language in the last twelve hours, but Mom just took the prize.

She sniffles, once, while she grips her hands together.

Put wall clocks on the list of things you never notice the sound of until the room goes awkwardly silent. I don't know if I'm supposed to guess what happened to my grandpa or ask for details. A coherent word doesn't get out of me before she answers my question.

"Your aunt and I were nineteen when Papa died. You know that much. Your grandma was at work. Rose and I just got back from shopping."

My ability to speak is slowly returning.

"Grandma Mutz . . ." I get out with effort. "She said he had a heart attack. In the bathroom." An image of my grandmother telling the tale conjures in my head. She never minded talking about it, even looked for times to bring it into conversation. She was always very matter-of-fact about it — would even say "death is a part of life."

"That may have been true. His heart did stop," she continues, "but only after he swallowed a bottle of his painkillers first."

No. Words.

"And that . . . that is what killed him."

All manners, grudges, or conversation etiquette is off the table. I'm saying what comes into my brain.

"But Grandma said he had a heart attack. She talks about it like it was just something that happens to people."

"Grandma wasn't the one who found him. I was." She doesn't hesitate that time.

The furnace kicks on to give the clock ticks some company. I'll gladly take any other noise as she continues.

"The bathroom door was open. He was on the floor with an empty pill bottle in the sink."

The remains of what was almost tears in her eyes are now gone. She is upright, determined to get this out. "And an envelope addressed to us was on his bed."

"What?" I'm down to one-syllable words. "Was it a note?"

She nods. "I called 911, but there was nothing they could do. He'd been dead for a while by the time we got home. He never went to work that day . . . just went into the bathroom and . . . and took all his medicine."

Wow. I had no idea. Of anything.

"But . . . then why did Grandma say he had a heart attack? Does she know?"

Mom nods, lips pursed.

"I called her and told her what happened. By the time she got home, the paramedics had taken him away. They tried to revive him, but he'd stopped breathing long before we found him. There was nothing anyone could do."

She looks at the floor again and exhales. "And . . ."

Another pause. I have a horrible feeling that my grandfather's secret death isn't the toughest thing she's had to say so far.

"Your grandma hugged me. She cried. I showed her the envelope." She pauses, seemingly to gather strength. "She grabbed me, shook me. And started yelling."

My head hurts. Picturing Grandma Mutz crying and yelling is crazy enough, but doing it over my grandfather's intentional overdose is too much. This doesn't make any sense.

"Why? Was she so upset he died?"

"Yes. But . . ." Mom looks down again. "She was also angry."

"At him?"

"At me. She ripped the envelope out of my hands. She grabbed me and yelled, 'His heart stopped and that's how he died!'" Her eyes find me again. "And told me I was never to say anything else."

The tear is returning.

"You didn't open it?"

Mom shakes her head, eyes still fixed on me.

"Do you know what it said?"

"No." Mom sits perfectly still. "To her, there was never a note."

"What about Aunt Rose?"

Mom's eyebrows go up slightly. She never forgets about her sister, but from the time she walked through my door, I think she had.

"Your aunt was there for it all, but she didn't say anything." She takes another deep breath. "She loved Papa very much, and I did, too." Mom tells me that last part sounding as if she almost forgot it. "But she wanted to have good memories of him, not the rest of it."

I don't understand "the rest of it," but can't bring myself to ask about it.

"So when your grandma told us his heart stopped, that's what your aunt believed, too."

"I . . ." No other words form. I struggle to get one more out. "Why?"

Mom looks at me again; her voice is calm.

"Sometimes, people don't want to see things because it's too difficult. Sometimes the bad is too much. So they see bad things how they want. They believe what they want."

She must be able to tell I'm even more confused. Between having never seen this side of my mother, never hearing about my grandfather's death, and never knowing my family had secrets . . . I'll take looking confused over my head exploding.

"They believe it until it becomes their reality."

Images of my family and how I know them are swirling in my head. And melting.

"Your grandma was a very good mother, but she didn't want to see her husband as someone who would end his own life. And she didn't want others to see him that way, either."

My mouth must be open.

"So I stayed quiet."

I should talk, but I have no response to any of this.

"I did what your grandma always taught us. I didn't interfere."

I sit still, wondering if this secret will get any bigger, as Mom's shoulders grow with a deep breath.

"She also didn't want to see her husband as some-one who wasn't the best father."

And there it is.

"He wasn't?" Another total shock. I knew he was tough on them and liked to drink, but not . . . not what-ever he was.

"He had a"— she searches for a descriptor to soften the blow of what she really wants to say —"a temper." She looks as though a particular memory of this tem-per is playing in her head. "And we never knew when it would come out. But when it did"— she inhales deeply —"it was bad."

Sounds like someone else we know.

Earlier today I looked at Greg Karlov with his father behind him and it reminded me of an apple and a tree. I can picture Patrick now, with my grandfather behind him.

"It was hard for us sometimes, living with him. He seemed to medicate himself more and more as he —"

She pauses, looks to the floor again.

"Rose and I . . . we looked out for each other."

Mom typically says what she means and means what she says, but not now. She's searching for every word. She takes another deep breath.

"He could yell so loud. Could get so angry. He was . . ." She stops. I don't know if she can find any more words.

"Scary."

It comes out of me without my even realizing it. Or realizing that I'm helping my mom right now.

"He was sick. We didn't know how to help him get better."

Her focus is back on me. She blinks hard, like she just woke up.

"So, like I said, I wanted to talk to you . . . about earlier," she replies, brushing her hands on her legs. "When you said that, about Patrick, it reminded me of some things I wanted to forget. And I reacted. Without realizing it."

Mom sighs and wipes her face. I don't think the day of talking to people at the wake compares to how exhausting the last few minutes were for her.

"Mom?"

"Yes."

"When was the last time you told that story?"

I can't explain why that question popped into my head, but it just spilled out. Mom's eyes get big. My question seems to make everything very real for her.

264

"Oh, wow," she gets out while sitting up straighter. "Before you were born. Before your father and I were married. That was the last"— another pause, this one with an expression of awareness —"the only time I ever told it."

I've never seen this . . . this vulnerable side of my mother.

"Jimmy, I don't want you to talk about this with anyone, all right? Some things are better left alone. OK?"

"Not even Aunt Rose?"

The worry of her fragile sister takes over her face. "Especially Aunt Rose."

"OK, I won't." Sometimes I tell Mom I'll do things just to appease her. I mean it this time.

"What you said about Patrick . . ." Another side-eye follows. "I don't think he intended for this to happen." She looks straight at me. "I really don't."

I honestly don't, either, and so regret saying it. I'm still a little afraid to respond, and decide to just listen.

"But he put himself in a spot where it did happen. And maybe he didn't even know why." She looks at the floor again.

I have never taken in so much information at once. I have no words at all. I think she senses the overload.

"OK, I think that's enough for today," Mom says with a nod. She places both palms on her knees and takes a quick breath. "You need to get to sleep. You ready for tomorrow?"

As crazy as hearing the family secret was, I appreciate the break from thinking about this speech.

"No. I can't think of anything to say." There's a difference in my voice now. I'm not complaining about the speech. I'm owning what I have to do. "I'll come up with something, though."

"All right. I'll let you finish, then." Mom stands up. She looks at the blank pad of paper, then back at me. "Don't stay up too late. You're only going to talk for two minutes tomorrow. Do you have any ideas?"

I look at the blank page with her. "No, but I'll make something up before tomorrow. I'll be fine."

"I know you will," she calmly replies while walking to my door. "And you can say whatever you want." She stops short of walking through the doorway and turns toward me.

"Don't make anything up."

*CHAPTER 11

If you're not sure what to say about the deceased, say it into a microphone.

I haven't been in many churches, but I feel like most of them have seedy-looking basements. Everything here has a tint of yellow, from the floors to the fold-up tables scattered across the room. Two older ladies in black suits are setting up a punch bowl that looks bigger than either of them. Dad said this is where the party is held after the service. I had no idea that people walked out of funerals and went straight to parties. It has to be better than the wake.

Mom and Aunt Rose are sitting in folding chairs talking quietly. Mom isn't holding her sister's hand;

one of the few times in the last three days that hasn't happened. Dad and Uncle Mike are sitting at a table next to them, looking around the room, with their legs stretched out and their hands in their pockets. Sofia is sitting with Norman and, like me, nervously waiting for what comes next in the mourning process.

This is it, my last chance to figure out what to say. I was too exhausted last night to write anything. Between the wake and hearing everything about my family, I couldn't keep my eyes open.

We should have a few more minutes before going up. I have to get something down. Mom said, "Don't make anything up," but I still want to be nice.

The crumpled paper finds its way out of my pocket again. It has to count this time. There's still one person I haven't consulted to create this speech.

OK, Patrick. What do you want me to say?
Something nice? How you'll be missed?
Or the truth?

Draft 3 of Speech

The truth is I never really tried.

I knew there was something wrong with him and I knew he couldn't always control it. Even when we were

*younger, I knew. I didn't need to be a detective to figure
out there was something rotten inside him the time
he punched my aunt in the mouth and yelled at her
afterward.*

*I did everything I could to keep away, but when he's
your cousin, and our moms are twins . . . only so much
distance is possible.*

*I told myself I tried to accept him. Instead I watched
the clock until he was gone.*

The truth is I'm kind of glad he's dead.

I can't say this!

I'm an awful person.

A third older woman comes down and pokes her
head in just long enough to say "It's time" before making an about-face and marching back upstairs.

I'm not ready. I'm not ready to speak. All I have
written down is what a horrible cousin I was. I'll pray
for a miracle. I'm already in church, so it can't hurt.
God, if you're listening, I want a tornado right now.

I know it's time for my cousin's funeral and I know
that's what I should be thinking about and I know that
I should feel sadder than I do . . . but I can't. It's time for
my speech and that's all I can think about. I can't focus

on anything but wanting this moment to be over with and how bad it'll be for everyone to have to hear it.

Uncle Mike gets up first. "Let's go," he whispers to his wife, who's now clutching Mom's hand. The five of us follow him up from the basement to where the stairs lead to the entryway of the church. Two men wearing black ties and a third man in a robe are waiting for us.

The priest. He looks toward the altar at the front of the church while the two men direct us where to go. I'm not sure he noticed we were there.

A pipe organ echoes through the walls. I don't know the song, but it makes me think of Halloween. The men in suits whisper something to Dad as he grabs my arm.

Oh, no. Are we going to be the first ones to walk in?

No? Oh, much worse. Everyone else is already here, seated, and waiting for us.

Dad leads me by the arm as we walk through the inner doors into a sea of eyes. Not one of them is looking to my much taller father, only at me. Some faces stream with tears, others just stare quizzically, but all of them are zeroed in on me.

They know.

They know I'm giving a speech and it's going to be awful.

We take step after step, splitting the church in half with every eye upon us. After passing each row, I pray our seat will be the next, so I can just sit down and not feel nine feet tall. Then I see the empty row we'll be claiming and I'm surprised again at what it means to be involved in a funeral.

I hate sitting near the front at church. I always feel like the priest is staring at me or thinking I did something bad. Or he's going to call on me to answer some question about John or Matthew or Michelangelo from the Old Testament to see if I know the Bible. No barrier between you and the man of the cloth means at any time he could take three steps and put you on the spot. I knew I was going to be on the spot today, and it makes me want to throw up even more.

Only when I turn to sit down am I aware that the rest of our group is right behind me.

Mom has her arm around her sister, shielding her from this quiet storm. Uncle Mike looks somber as ever as he leads his daughter and Norman to our row.

Each of us stands patiently in our place, looking back for the priest to make his entrance. He proceeds slowly toward the altar and stops at the casket.

Patrick. I've been so crazed about speaking that I

didn't even notice he was here. In the center of the aisle, with a massive arrangement of flowers and ribbons hanging down from the top, is the casket housing my cousin.

The priest makes the sign of the cross in front of the casket. After walking to the side and up the two steps to the altar, he stands over the audience and pauses before moving again. He has some kind of cloth he begins folding. But he does it slowly. Like he knows everyone's watching and he doesn't care how much time he takes. He places both of his palms on the altar. I look at my hands as they tremble, clasping together. His hands lie perfectly still while he stares at something on the altar that none of us is seeing. The priest straightens up, takes a breath, and begins to speak.

This is it. The moment I truly fear. Hearing the priest's voice means at some point in the next hour he'll say "And now Patrick's cousin will give a speech" or something like that. Then it's over for me.

He gives an opening prayer of some kind. Everyone here seems to know what to do except me. With the sign of the cross again, his hand gestures for the audience to be seated. OK, at least I'm not starting this. And at least everyone is going to sit down first, and hopefully he'll talk longer. I reach for the wooden bench and gladly take my sea —

What was that?

My pants.

NO. Not now.

The button.

It popped.

Not now! Not now in front of everyone. Not now when I'm going to have to walk in front of everyone!

I've never been this nervous in my life. I'm aware of every detail around me and also completely unable to process anything. I know the priest is talking, but I'm only hearing disconnected words. I'm a mess. A train wreck. At any moment, I'll be called up to give a speech about Patrick and I have no —

What?

The priest is looking at me. Focus. Memories . . . Why we're here . . . Oh, no. This is it? Can't be. It just started. Isn't he going to bless us first or say some kind of prayer?

"And we have young James, who is going to share a memory of Patrick, whom we are here to celebrate today."

I only hear "James" and know I'm done for.

He turns to sit in a large wooden chair at the back of the platform.

Does that mean come up? Celebrate? Why would anyone use the word "celebrate" at a funeral? I can't move. Completely frozen from my neck down, I pray that the priest was just talking about me and not telling me to come up to "celebrate" yet. Dad squeezes my arm and whispers, "Go on, you'll do fine."

It's time.

I stand. Too terrified to look back at the masses behind me, I focus on the bottom step leading to the podium before moving on.

My pants . . . Why now? How did I wear these all day yesterday and not break them?

My jacket . . . That's it! I can button my jacket and hold my hand where the button was and no one will notice. I just have to make it to the podium and it will conceal my zipper coming undone.

I button my jacket with one hand while clasping my pants with the other.

This can't be happening! I can't have my pants fall off in front of everyone.

Almost there. Up two steps and don't turn around

until you're directly behind the podium. At the top. Almost.

The pants will stay if I'm only standing and not moving. Three more steps and I'm there. *Now turn, and I'm safe.*

I make it. I can keep still while I talk and no one will know.

The mic is way too high. I pull it down carefully so as not to dislodge it from the silver neck. I succeed in keeping the mic in one piece, but it was not worth the cringe-inducing sound of a car accident in slow motion that came over the speakers. I can't think of a worse way to start a speech than to fill the room with high-decibel bending of metal.

I look over the crowd from the front of the church and two steps higher than everyone, and it's a completely different room. And bigger. Somehow the laws of physics are bent when you give a speech, and the room lengthens by twice as much. And the people, at least four times as many as it looked like from the back.

I take a long, exaggerated breath and realize something. For the first time in the last twenty-four hours, I have space.

No one is near me. No one is talking to me. No one is even at my level as I look out above everyone else.

It feels . . . good. I take another breath. The button popping off my pants may have actually been the miracle I prayed for.

I can breathe.

Never mind the awkward silence; I need this. No one is shaking my hand, no one is talking to me, and no one is asking me where I was when Patrick died.

I stand with as much phony confidence a thirteen-year-old boy about to speak publicly at his dead cousin's funeral can muster, and manage to get the first word out.

"Patrick . . ."

One word.

Staring down at the wooden podium, I begin the task that has dominated my thoughts through all the chaos. Another breath, this one bigger than the last, and my chest is full for what feels like the first time in days. One more and I'll let the words go with it.

Don't make anything up. . . .

A string of syllables comes out. I don't even realize what I said until the church collectively gasps.

By then it's too late.

*CHAPTER 12

Listen more than you speak.

"Patrick was kind of an asshole."

Holy balls. I said it. Did I actually say out loud what I'd thought about Patrick since preschool? When I see Grandma Mutz's eyes get big enough to pop in the second row, I know the words escaped. No manners, no filter, no holding back — just my actual thoughts.

I take another breath. And it feels amazing.

"Ever since I've known him, I've never understood him. I've never understood why he did the things he did or why he acted the way he did."

I look to my family. Dad is leaning forward a bit but hasn't committed to taking me offstage yet. I can tell he's just as curious as he is worried about where I'm going with this. Thing is . . . I don't know. I have no idea what the next sentence is going to be.

I'm . . . I'm being heard.

I've never been here before.

It feels good.

"So I thought . . . I thought he was doing it on purpose."

The words begin to flow into the mic as I keep breathing and talking. I'm not yelling. I'm not angry, or even frustrated. I'm just telling everyone what I've learned.

"I remember things about Patrick from when we were younger. I remember that if I ever got a new toy, I needed to hide it because Patrick would break it. And if I ever got ice cream in the summer, Patrick would find a way to make me drop it."

I scan the crowd. Most of the mouths have closed at this point, but everyone is sitting straighter. A woman from the neighborhood is gripping her husband's arm, whispering what I'm sure is concern. I take an odd pleasure in seeing her six rows back, and her husband is totally focused on me. I have the mic, and no one is listening to her.

"Once he got mad at me for choosing Rocky Road. He didn't know what Rocky Road was and got strawberry. He was furious when he saw mine had marshmallows. He tripped me and made it look like an accident. Then he said he fell, too, and was hurt so he wouldn't get in trouble. That's the Patrick I knew. That's the Patrick I remember." I feel myself stand taller. I'm pretty sure no one's ever heard a funeral speech like mine.

I inhale again.

"When we were in kindergarten, he told me that hot salsa was just fancy ketchup and I should put a lot of it on my hot dog. I did, and cried for an hour because my tongue wouldn't stop burning. I still haven't eaten it since then. He ruined salsa for me."

It's spilling out of me.

"He ruined a lot of things for me."

I know it's wrong and I know I'm here to be respectful, but it feels so good to exhale with what I was never allowed to say. I keep going and feel my eyes well up.

"I tried so hard to be nice to him . . ."

It's starting to feel different now. My breathing is too

deep. My chest is starting to hurt the way it did when I was cornered at the wake. I realize something new. I'm stuck up here, with nowhere to go.

"I don't know what else to say."

For the first time since standing behind the podium, I look at Patrick's family. I didn't want to see them at first. I'm not sure why; I just know I didn't. Aunt Rose has a tissue wadded in her free hand, but she stopped crying. Her face has an expression as if she's hearing about her son for the first time. Uncle Mike looks like I've never seen him before. He looks scared.

But Sofia . . .

"That's what I remember about Patrick." The words are coming again. "I remember knowing that if he was around, something bad was going to happen."

Oh, no, please don't start crying. . . .

"Many of you thought we were friends. We were never really friends."

Getting harder to breathe . . .

"I don't think he even liked me."

Oh, no. The tears.

"He . . . I . . ."

The words stop coming. What do I do? I try my best to fight back the tears, but they begin to squeak out.

The podium suddenly feels like a very lonely place, a place I no longer want to be.

I need an exit. I need to end this speech. I'm pretty sure I've already lost my audience. They're no longer listening to me.

No one is even looking at me.

Their eyes are on Sofia.

I don't know how much of what I said Sofia understood. She didn't need to hear any of it, though. She saw I was losing it.

Her footsteps fall silent as she makes her way to the podium with Norman in tow. The eyes of the church follow, and my sweet little cousin now stands next to me and takes my hand. Her focused gaze to the seated spectators tells them what I'd been trying to say for the last two days; I needed help.

Sofia heard me.

Norman, Sofia, and me. I bet no one in this room ever thought the three of us would be standing behind a microphone silencing an audience. My chest eases up; my breathing slows a bit. I look down at my protector, standing guard to my right. She never looks at me. Instead, her gaze is now locked on the casket with her brother inside.

She knew. She knew what we were all afraid to see.

I regain my voice as much as possible.

"I know why, though." One more controlled breath. "I know why Patrick never liked me."

Just like before, the words are out before my thought is complete. This breath I don't so much enjoy but, rather, need.

"I never listened to him."

My eyes find Patrick's casket as a sniffle comes from the back of the church.

"Ever."

A whimper comes from the front. When I glance at my family, they no longer look worried about what I'll say.

"Patrick talked a lot. He always had something to say. But I never listened to him."

Small breath.

"I could have —"

Inhale.

"But I didn't."

That is the first time I've seen my father cry.

"I could've offered to help him, but I didn't. I wasn't listening." I look at the casket again. The rest of the church is erased from my vision. I only see the shining beige box with the body of my cousin, and a wave of reality sets in.

I'll never see Patrick again.

"I wasn't listening to you."

Even with Sofia holding me up with her tiny hand, I can't do this much longer.

"I know you were telling me something was wrong. And I didn't listen."

I take one more breath to make the words resonate. These words are going to be heard.

"Patrick, I'm sorry."

Sofia grips my hand tighter. She doesn't know what I'm saying, but something's caused her to want to hold on to someone. I see her parents and it makes sense. It wasn't my aunt wiping tears off her cheeks. It was my uncle. His face is covered by his hands.

"I'm sorry." The high pitch that only heightened emotion brings out of my voice finds its way again. I'm focusing, more than I thought possible, on getting complete sentences out. "I didn't hear you."

It's the first time I've seen my uncle cry.

"Patrick, you taught me . . ."

This is it. I don't have much left in me.

"You taught me to listen."

I look to my family and see Mom's face, completely focused on me.

Her eyes aren't wet. She doesn't look sad.

She looks proud.

"I promise from now on, I will."

Sofia looks at me. She's seen my lips and heard me talk to her brother. I squeeze her hand to say thank you. She knows I mean it. I hold the top of my buttonless pants and we step away from the podium. She guides me as we walk hand in hand down the steps to rejoin the rest of the family.

It's over. My speech is finished, my Odyssey complete. I was so overwhelmed by it, though, I forgot something. Everyone in the room forgot something.

Sofia hasn't said good-bye to her brother yet.

Before we reach our families, Sofia stops and lets go of my hand. My feet stay in place. I won't sit down without her. The entire church watches, waiting to see what this silent little girl will do.

With her back to the crowd, Sofia stands tall in front of the long casket, the top of her head lined up with the white flowers resting on the lid. She puts her hand on the side of her brother's coffin, only her fingertips touching. She doesn't move, doesn't cry, and doesn't make a sound. What she's saying to her brother in this moment only Patrick and Sofia know.

In the crook of her other arm, locked tight against her chest, is Norman. She lets him out of the hold and stands on her highest toes to reach the top of the casket, while raising the walrus over her head. With an extra-effort bounce, Norman is placed on the casket over Patrick's heart. She returns to her heels for one last look at her walrus.

She's giving Norman to her brother. Norman, who always made her feel safer, is now going to look out for Patrick.

Sofia turns to me. Her eyes are so tired. She walks through her new, glistening tears until her hand finds mine.

In all the awful small talk I had to endure over the last twenty-four hours, it never once occurred to me to ask Patrick's sister if she was OK. I grip her delicate hand tightly, letting her know I am listening now. Neither of us has been here before, but we're here together.

Sofia and I take our seats as the priest stands back at the podium. He continues with the rest of the funeral as scheduled. Other than a few words about Patrick, the service is basically sitting through normal church. Had it not been for the casket in the front, someone walking in would've never known it was a funeral. I thought it would be different. I don't know how, just different.

My speech is over, though. I have no idea how it was received. I just know I never could've said it without my cousin Sofia.

The only one who ever listened to Patrick.

Sofia always wanted a kitten. She loved cats. They fit her personality well: quiet, caring, and mildly passive-aggressive. She asked for one every Christmas and never had that wish fulfilled. I always suspected my aunt and uncle were too worried about the life span of an animal with Patrick in the house.

When it was Sofia's turn to open her birthday gift from Patrick, her wish was granted. Kind of.

Patrick swore he would get her a pet (a bold promise for a nine-year-old), and she was certain a kitten awaited her. Still on her knees, she peered into the box and her expression changed. Her eyes were alive as she ripped the paper off. When she opened the box, she looked more like she was doing long division in her head.

It wasn't a kitten.

She reached in to pull out a portly long-toothed walrus. It wasn't very fluffy for a stuffed animal, or even very cute. Patrick excitedly waited for her response, as if an ugly walrus were at the top of her wish list. Sofia smiled at this and hugged her new seaworthy friend. She named him Norman and she rarely left the house without him.

After that birthday, Patrick developed this skit he always did with Norman.

He'd sit on his bed, across from Sofia, with the walrus on his lap. He'd patiently pet him, as if the stuffed animal were a purring cat and only he could keep Norman calm. Sofia would show a toothy grin, knowing the show was starting. This was the first of many performances I'd seen.

Patrick wasn't skilled at many things, but puppetry was something he excelled at. Norman wasn't a puppet, just an ordinary stuffed animal. But somehow Patrick could maneuver his fingers around the neck to make him lifelike. Sofia was always positioned in front, so she didn't see much of his fingers. When Patrick convinced her that Norman was calm enough to listen, the walrus would start performing.

"Hi, Norman! How're you? What? Is something wrong?" Norman's role was always something like a shy party guest. I have no idea where Patrick got this. He always displayed terrible manners.

He maneuvered Norman to crawl up his arm and nestle in his shirt like the animal was too scared to answer. "It's OK." He looked at Sofia. "Her? She's not scary. She wants to talk to you, Norman. Do you want to meet Sofia?"

Sofia sat up straighter, pretending she had never met her own pet walrus. Norman's head shook with vigor while his lengthy front teeth bobbed left and right.

"Awwwww, are you scared? Sofia won't hurt you." Norman lifted his head and locked eyes with Patrick. "I promise. She'll be very nice to you. You think you could say hi?"

Norman's head took a bashful downward-facing nod. His right flipper moved up slightly to wave hello to Sofia. Patrick not only had the motions down, but the timing. A perfect pause came before each movement that only sold this story more.

Sofia smiled so you could see all her teeth. She was never shy to ask for what she wanted. Her hands typically moved at a brisk pace to speak her mind. Not now. Her hands lay still, fearing any sudden movement would scare Norman off.

"Go ahead, Sofia. Say hi," Patrick said, instructing his sister. She obediently followed with a gentle wave, then returned her hands to a still position.

"Norman, did you want to show us your dance?" Norman's head was looking up at Patrick, and then slowly reverted back to the bashful pose. Patrick tapped his hand on his leg, a subtle way to get his sister to look at his lips. "Sofia, do you want to see him dance?"

She nodded excitedly while rocking in her place. It was as though he had a giant hand behind his sister as well.

I was convinced Patrick practiced this when no one was around. He was able to control both of Norman's flippers with his thumb and pinky finger while moving the walrus's head with the rest of his hand. Being a stuffed animal in a fixed sitting position, Norman was pretty limited in his range of motion. But Patrick could somehow make his movements so lifelike that I couldn't stop watching.

He had a little routine: three bops of the head and the left flipper went up like a dancer's in a kickline. Then three bops again and the right flipper. Patrick hummed a little song for the dance. He knew Sofia couldn't hear it, but he did it anyway. Sofia's wide eyes took in every movement.

After a few sets on each side, the big finish came with both of Norman's flippers up. Sofia applauded wildly. Norman bowed and went back to his bashful stance.

"What's wrong, Norman?"

I never heard empathy in Patrick's voice except when he talked to this walrus that wasn't real. Norman was shaking his head while trying to hide, almost shamefully. I knew the stuffed animal didn't have a shameful expression, but that's how good Patrick was.

He tapped his leg again.

"Oh, I know." He leaned in closer to the shy animal and looked at his sister. "Did you want to give Sofia a hug? Let me see if she wants one."

Sofia's back went straight up, matching her eyebrows. She put her hands on her knees and waited for a response.

Norman looked up at Sofia for the first time. The walrus, after another perfectly timed pause, made his way down Patrick's leg (as best he could since only his front flippers moved). He stopped again at Patrick's knee, looking up at Sofia. Her hands fluttered slightly — not in a sweet way, more of a scared way. It reminded me of that reflex game where you hold your hands above someone else's and they try to slap them.

Patrick had Sofia. He had me. Both of us leaned in, waiting to see what this bashful, talented sea creature would do.

Then Sofia blinked.

Norman launched off Patrick's leg with speed he'd kept hidden. He didn't hop or bounce. He made a bullet-straight shot for his target, the side of Sofia's neck. Patrick spoke for Norman now, his voice having taken on that of a grizzly bear attacking its prey. He snarled and growled while forcing what I thought was the most gentle animal on earth to lunge at the throat of my innocent cousin. My shoulders moved back on their own. I was caught completely off guard. Sofia was now on her back with her hands around a feral walrus attacking her jugular.

I was about to help, if not for the sound that came out of Sofia.

Her laugh. Her laugh was so rarely heard and never

like this. Even though Norman had her throat, it couldn't stop the sound coming from deep in her belly. She squirmed and wriggled to get away, but it was no use. Much like Patrick knew how to manipulate this toy walrus, he also knew how his sister would react. After a few more seconds, Sofia was struggling to find her breath from laughing so hard, and Patrick knew it was time to call off the beast.

He never had any intention of making Norman hug his sister. That's why Sofia was flinching and batting her hands — she knew this was coming. She'd been here before.

Patrick sat up on the bed as if nothing had happened. Norman was sitting between them, a regular stuffed animal again. Sofia caught her breath and sat up. She brushed her now-tangled hair to the side and made a C with her hand while bringing it to her open palm. She repeated this gesture at a frenzied pace until her brother responded.

Patrick broke character as he addressed his sister.

"OK, OK," he said while situating Norman on his knee. I sat quietly while the walrus returned to his original withdrawn stance.

Sofia continued with her motions, eyes wide, waiting for her brother's response.

"Again. I know."

He smiled and relaxed his shoulders.

"I heard you."

ADAM P. SCHMITT has been a middle-school educator for more than fifteen years. *Speechless* is his debut middle-grade novel, about which he says, "This story came to me in a single moment while at the funeral of a former student. It's sadly not the only service for a student I've attended. The characters here don't represent any one person, but several people in my life who had stories to tell and didn't know how to find someone to listen." Adam P. Schmitt lives in Oswego, Illinois, with his wife and two sons.